PIRATE'S TREASURE

PIRATE'S TREASURE

TRIANGLE OF SPIRITS BOOK ONE

Austin Ryan

To Mormor,

Inger=Annÿ Wattum

for our friendship, for believing in me always,

and for all the days when the one thing

that kept me from giving up, was knowing

you were proud of me.

Table of Contents

CHAPTER 1

The woods call to us with a hundred voices, but the sea has one only — a mighty voice that drowns our souls in its majestic music. The woods are human, but the sea is of the company of the archangels.
—L. M. MONTGOMERY

Tress

New England, 2019

*L*ove *doesn't last forever. You need to stop living in a fairytale, Tress."*

Jonah's words ring in my ears as the mournful cries of seagulls echo the ache in my chest.

Waves break against the large, darkened boulders, and the whipped foam fizzles over smaller rocks. I savor the rumbling sound of the great unknown calling me to adventure.

"You? An adventurer?"

Jonah had laughed, but he'd been right. I am no adventurer.

If I had been, would he have stayed? Would they all have stayed?

Or was I never the kind of girl worth staying for?

My life isn't a fairytale. The world has tried to wash away my dreams too many times for that. I've kept my head above the water, but I owe my sanity to the stories that held me together when the world did its best to tear me apart.

The stories that still hold me together.

Along with this place.

Within earshot of the rumbling waves, where the smell of saltwater and seaweed permeates the air, I feel the closest thing I've ever felt to home.

It's been more than two decades since my big brother first started taking me here to get us both away from the wrath of our parents.

The wind coming off the wide expanse of water ruffles my hair—lifting it up, dropping it gently back down on my shoulders.

I tug my phone out of my pocket and pull my eyes away from the white capped waves. I'm late for my shift at the library.

I scramble off my rock and run to my car.

But even as I shut the car door, the pungent air fills the space around me. I breathe in the ocean air, and every breath in this place feels like destiny. Destiny that rides on the waves as much as the salty foam.

It's coming for me.

I feel it in my bones.

The morning rush has come and gone, and the library lobby is sunlit and empty. I bend over the cart of returned books and scan the titles for anything of interest. I'm always on the lookout for my next reader's high.

I pick up a promising volume and flick through the pages. A sci-fi fantasy Cinderella retelling. I put it on the desk, then kneel to study the titles on the bottom shelf of the cart.

I drop a bright teal book I find next behind the counter and shove the cart in front of me across the lobby and toward the mystery section. Just three of the books belong there, but it seems as good of a place to start as any.

I scan the shelves for the exact spot of the tome in my hand.

Laughter trickles through the still air of the first floor.

Usually I love the laughter and snippets of conversation trickling out from between the shelves, but this laughter is too familiar.

A ripple of unease flits through my stomach, and I glance back towards the lobby.

A young couple is tangled up together next to the library book-sale shelf. They break their kiss, and my stomach roils.

I'm in no way against public displays of affection. Normally I'm highly in favor. But I don't want to glimpse this couple's full-on library makeout session.

The man trails a hand around his girlfriend's waist, and my stomach turns. His thick fingers come to rest on her hip, and I can't seem to tear my eyes away from them.

His face is turned away from me, but I already know the look in his eyes. Because this man used to look at me the same way.

His strong, tanned fingers used to flirt with the edge of my shirt, and I used to wiggle away just like the blonde girl is now.

Lucas.

I watch the scene unfold, and something breaks inside me. Its jagged edges rip at the flesh of my heart, drawing fresh blood from a wound that was nearly healed.

Or did I only think it was healed?

Maybe all that was healed was the scab of an older wound that ran much deeper?

My stomach knots. I want so badly to look away.

They can't see me now, but if they walk up to the counter I will have to wait on them. Because that's my job.

Unless I'm on a different floor.

I tear my eyes away from Lucas and his girlfriend, and half run, half stumble towards the nearest elevator, pulling the return cart behind me.

Some of these books have to belong in the basement.

I saw at least a copy of *Jane Eyre*, and there's a Bronte sister display on one of the end caps down there.

I clutch on to this feeble reason to abandon my post as I stop in front of the metal doors of my escape.

I press the button, and an eternity passes before the loud descent of the elevator overpowers the deep, rumbling laugh that makes my knees feel weak and the throaty giggles that are no longer mine.

The elevator lowers me and my cart of books into the belly of the library, and my thoughts flit to last spring.

Lucas had been a mistake from day one. Not because

he had been wrong for me. Lucas had been very right. Jonah had taken back the ring that all my hopes and dreams had hinged on four years before I met Lucas. I still hadn't been ready.

Falling in love when your heart wasn't in it apparently only worked in books, and Lucas had gotten tired of waiting.

How can it hurt so bad still, when my missing feelings led to the breakup?

The elevator screeches to a halt, and the books in my cart shift with the movement.

"Lasting love is a fairytale, Tress. Don't you know that?"

Jonah's words had resounded in my head as I'd watched Lucas walk away, and my resolve to stay away from love had sharpened a hundredfold.

Love is not for you.

I glance at the books in my cart again as I wait for the doors to open.

In the stories contained in this library, I am the heroine whose husband kisses her tenderly before leaving for work in the fields.

I am the mother within the pages singing her babies to sleep.

In my imagination I have found a place to belong.

And as long as I let my castle of dreams stay between the covers of one book after another, it can never again come crashing down.

The elevator doors open, and I push the rickety book cart into the room.

The one copy of *Jane Eyre* is a flimsy excuse to be down here. Chris might be more a friend than a supervisor, but I don't know that she'll let this slide. Still, I'm willing to chance Chris's lecture to avoid a reminder of my failed relationship.

I kneel in front of the cart and look through the titles again, a little more thoroughly this time. The volume called *Seafaring Through the Ages* does indeed belong down here.

I let out a breath of relief.

Leaving the cart where it is, I grab the large book and the copy of *Jane Eyre* and head to the shelves that form the long aisles cutting across the room.

A familiar scent wafts through the room, one that doesn't at all belong here.

My senses must be playing tricks on me, because instead of the tantalizing mixture of leather, ink, and paper, I swear I can smell the ocean.

I shove *Seafaring Through the Ages* into its spot on the shelf.

I close my eyes, and I can almost taste the salt on my lips.

I open my eyes and follow the sound of breaking waves, creaking wood, and faint...singing?

A crash cracks the air in the still room, and the noise of rushing water drowns out any other sound.

I take the corner at a run.

Piercing eyes meet mine, and I stop dead.

CHAPTER 2

Charles

The Atlantic Ocean, 1725

The dark clouds rolling over the horizon don't bide well.

"Keep the course steady. I don't think we can outrun this one."

"Yes, Captain."

Lightning flashes in the distance as my first mate makes his way back to take the wheel from me.

His frown is telling. Will Hayle is not a man who lets a scowl sit useless on his face.

All afternoon Lady Monroe's sails have been filled with brisk wind, moving us at a great clip.

But the darkness that closes in on us from the East is more than I'd bargained for. The first raindrops hit the deck, and their rapidly increasing cadence feels like a warning.

Unease clenches in my stomach, matching my frown.

Lady Monroe has weathered many a storm, but the die isn't yet cast with this one.

I order the lookout to come down from the crow's nest as the first sheet of rain whips across the ship. He scoots down the wet rigging until he's safely on deck.

Wind tears at the ship around us and a relentless rain soaks every crewman struggling with lines and sails.

Darkness sinks over us as thick canvas tears and the unrelenting wind wrecks the first sail.

I bark the order to lower the sail and watch as the crew scramble to obey it, but I know it's too late for that one.

We'll have to manage without it.

"This storm is going to pull us off course, Captain!"

Will's words are a warning, but I know it already. I feel it in my bones. Destiny asks for no man's approval, and she's coming for my ship.

Within the hour, ungodly howls tear through the air, and without consulting the map in the cabin I know where we are.

The Triangle of Spirits—cursed waters from which few sailing ships ever return.

Freezing rain soaks my clothes and skin as reality sinks in.

I've heard stories of ships disappearing never to be seen again, of ghostly apparitions making whole crews go mad. Men falling overboard only to disappear from the surface without going under.

The Lady Monroe groans as towering waves toss her to and fro. The scent of terror fills the air. Even fearless pirates know to fear these waters.

Crewmen climb the slippery ropes of the rigging looking more like monkeys than men. Traversing the foot ropes below the rain slicked yardarms, they work quickly with fingers that must already be numb with cold.

A shriek sounds over the storm, turning the heads of men on deck. McDilly's long limbs flail and grab onto the last line of rope between him and a fall that will cut short his hopes of retiring a gentleman of fortune. If he even falls to the deck.

The tension in my shoulders doesn't cease when he makes a return to standing and is yet again hunched over the yardarm, arms full of wet and heavy canvas.

When the torn sail is stowed, he steps onto the deck, holding on to the ratline for support and with a face as pale as death.

Barely a lad of twenty, his shoulders don't have the width of a man yet, but they carry the burden of one. He has a wife and an infant at home.

Will they mourn him if he doesn't make it out of the Triangle? Or will his wife do like the woman who promised to be mine—move on without a second thought?

A wave rises on the starboard side of the Lady Monroe.

"Hold on to your lines!"

I curl my arm around the line strung up next to me, and when the wave washes over the railing and crashes onto the deck, my feet disappear under me from the force of the icy water.

The coarse rope bites into my flesh with bruising force, and the air is nothing but white seaspray. I close my mouth and wait for the air to be breathable again. But even then the call of "Man overboard" never sounds.

All my men have heard the stories of the Triangle. The few crewmen who have made it back out with their wits intact tell of unimaginable terrors. But though they may be laughed off in a tavern, at sea, surrounded by forces that border the unnatural, the story is different.

"Hail Mary, Mother of God—"

My feet find footing again on the slick deck just as an ear-splitting crack sounds from above, and I don't think even Hail Marys will save us now.

Hand over hand on coarse rope, I make my way back to the quarter deck and my first mate.

A deathly quiet sinks over the ship. Then another crack of thunder. A flash of lightning.

"—now and at the hour of our death."

"You know you're in poor shape when you hear prayers aboard a pirate vessel!"

Will shouts the words in the brief stillness between crashes overhead.

He's not wrong.

Will and I first set foot aboard a ship when we were barely lads of fifteen, and we've sailed together ever since.

He knows I had charted a course well around these dreaded waters, and that the summer squall on the horizon shouldn't have made a lick of difference.

But another tearing of the heavens above us drowns out every other sound, and it seems fate wants it differently.

Will's expression is grim, and by his and Mose's white knuckled grip on the hands of the wheel, they both know as well as I do that our chances of making it out of this are slim.

Hour after hour passes in the near darkness of the storm as I work as one with my crew. Foaming sea water keeps washing across the deck as it tilts from one side to the other as the Lady Monroe is tossed to and fro in the waves.

Boots slide across the deck planks as crewmen run to fulfill my orders.

The wet rope tears blisters from my skin as it slips through my hands and the hands of the row of men behind me.

"Hold!"

The rope stills at my shout.

I look up in time to see the terrified face of my cabin boy staring back at me from where he has a death grip on the door that leads to the crew's quarters.

"Go below!"

He nods his head and scurries below deck, and I let out a breath of relief.

We haven't lost a single man yet, and I want to keep it that way.

"Keep the sails low!"

I bellow my orders to the crewmen closest to me, and still my words are faint like whispers above the loud groans from the wood and rigging.

"Fix!"

The crewman's hand that fastens the rope around the pin pull is torn and bloody, and his is far from the only one.

I look around me and know the men on deck are only still standing from sheer strength of character.

But will it be enough to keep the Lady Monroe, and our bodies, from ending up on the bottom of the sea?

The pallid faces and still muttered prayers around me testify that where we are now might be worse. I've seen men's faces pale in memory of the horrors of this place. And now I know why.

The gale takes up force around us, and we descend into a place that may well be the entrance to hell.

I clamber my way from the main mast to the quarterdeck.

The ship shakes with the forces of the underworld, and the loud prayers around me turn fervent, desperate.

Will makes no move to speak as he steps aside. His eyes are red from the wind and salt, and there are no prayers on his lips.

Death comes for all men, but I've never known a man who *lived* more than Will.

My fingers curl around the handles of the wheel, and I bid farewell to the world.

For a moment in time, the bellow of the storm around us rises until it must end—so terrifying is the sound.

Then, as swiftly as it appeared on the horizon, the thunder and lightning ceases.

The whipping wind quiets.

The hammering rain turns to a drizzle.

The raging gale turns to steadily rocking waves.

My heart expands in my chest as the first fiery light of the new day trickles out from the heavy clouds. Like a glowing benediction over a crew dead on their feet. Relief sinks through my bones.

Will lets out a long breath next to me.

"I didn't think..."

He doesn't finish his words—experienced seafarers know not to speak ill luck upon their ships, but I hear the surprise in his voice. The disbelief.

We shouldn't have made it through this storm, not without a miracle.

Is this one?

I drop a hand on Will's broad shoulder, and his clasps down on top of mine.

"We wouldn't have made it without you."

It's our creed from years ago, one we haven't spoken for years.

The truth of it settles into muscles shaking from strain, and hearts that nearly—no, that did—give up.

The lookout crawls back up to his crow's nest, his face as gray as the rest of the crew's. There is no cheer rising over the victory we've had over Poseidon, just quiet nods and shaking legs.

And when the sun braces golden on the horizon, it's over a crew and ship worse for wear, but not a single man has been lost.

I leave the wheel to Will and descend the ladder leading below deck.

The Lady Monroe tilts gently back and forth with the movement of the ocean. I have spent the better half of my life at sea, and the movement of the vessel beneath my feet is as natural as if I had never been used to ground that didn't move.

The waves' steady thump against the hull of the ship settle me as I enter my quarters. I stride across the room and light the hanging lamp above to disperse the glow in the still dark cabin. I grab a rolled-up map, spread it out on my desk, and place weights at both ends. Then I study the map again.

The course I had charted was to have pulled us east of the dreaded Triangle of Spirits. I had feared we were still close enough to the dangerous waters that stormy weather could push us into them. And the collection of dark clouds my lookout had glimpsed on the horizon had proved me right.

The soft light from the lamp shifts with the movements of the ship, and a dark shape wedged between the wall and the heavy desk catches my eye.

I reach for it, and my fingers brush soft leather. But I can't get close enough to grasp it.

I curl my hands around both edges of the heavy desk and pull it forward. It barely moves.

I let out a curse that lives up to the reputation of sailors and push on the desk again. When I reach down this time, my fingers grip the object firmly, pulling it out into the yellow light of the oil lamp.

It's a book. Heavy and bound in soft leather. Golden letters grace the front of it.

I open it and find lines of tidy script that mean nothing to me. But even an illiterate sea captain can appreciate the craftsmanship that has gone into the making of the volume.

It isn't my book, for the sole reason that I don't own any. My cabin boy writes out my captain's log, and other than maps and constellations, I have no use for reading.

I place the book on my desk and go back to studying the map before me.

But the book taunts me from its place on the edge of my desk.

There was a time when I did spend hours in the company of books. When the woman I called mine read as well as a man.

All my sailing up to that point had been for petty coin spent as soon as we made port and reduced to nothing but heady memories by the time we left again. But with her sweet promises ringing in my ears, my goal shifted to providing a home, a living. For her, and someday, our children.

I glare at the book, but it does nothing to dispel my thoughts.

Sarah Monroe knew how to decipher the marks in her father's leather-bound books. She'd read me stories rivaling the many I'd come to experience later. Her deceptive smile still haunts my dreams.

It's not a mistake I'll make again.

I close my eyes to keep the memories at bay, but they play in my mind without invitation.

I'm spellbound as her soft voice fills the parlor in her father's house as she reads. Then her pealing laughter does the

19

same, the moment her maid leaves and I wrestle the book from her and take her in my arms.

I grind my teeth as the memory of her laughter taunts me from beyond the grave.

Perhaps if I'd been able to pen a letter home she wouldn't have ceased waiting. Wouldn't have married a blacksmith whose career was firmly on land. A man who could warm her bed every night, not leaving her cold and lonely waiting for my return.

If I could have sent her word perhaps she wouldn't have died bearing his child.

Or maybe she'd have died bearing yours.

My eyes rest again on the vaguely triangular shape on the map spread across my desk, as if my consciousness is drawn by one tragedy to another.

The drawings on the map are sinister.

"Storms never leave the place. It is cursed. Cursed! Any captain wanting to make it back to shore will do well to avoid it!"

The old sailor's words ring in my ears like they did when I visited my first tavern with coins to spend.

I have never doubted his words. And in the fifteen years that have passed since, I've never seen evidence to the contrary. Jack Morgan and his crew were never heard from again after sailing too close a decade ago. One man of Samuel Redd's crew made it back. His wits never returned.

And somehow, the Lady Monroe, and her crew, is still intact. We have made it through, minds and bodies.

I roll the map up and replace it in the wooden receptacle, extinguish the light, and leave my cabin behind.

"Captain, sir. Do you need anything?"

The thin voice stops me just as a dark shape scrambles to a stand next to me. In the early morning light from the open doorway to the deck my cabin boy's face looks green under his freckles.

I shake my head.

"Get some rest."

The lad is barely the age I was when I had his position. It may be many years ago, but I still remember the way my stomach roiled after my first storm.

And what a storm to traverse as your first.

Back on deck, I oversee the mending of the sails.

I replace the man at the helm and keep an eye on any signals from my lookout. As battered as the Lady Monroe is right now, we don't need any surprises.

But we don't get any.

When the sun is high in the skies, the battering storm is but a memory, and the crew's shanties again rise from the deck.

Leaving the wheel to Will, I make my way through the doorway of my cabin, dead on my feet.

I have all but forgotten the book sitting on my captain's desk. It's still there, prodding my memory of my first love. And my deepest betrayal.

As if drawn there, my eyes fasten on it.

It bursts open. I throw up a hand to shield my face, but as I seek it out again, the light burns my eyes. Fumbling in the blinding whiteness, I take a step forward and reach for the book.

If I can close its pages, I can rid my cabin of this ungodly light.

And then, I'm suspended in mid-air. The sounds of my surroundings reach me louder than before.

The dull thumping of waves against the hull, the deep baritones of my crew.

The musty smell of my cabin fades for a fainter smell I can't place.

Then I'm submerged in water. Pulled underneath in a current so strong it leaves me unable to move. When I can breathe again, my boots hit soaked carpet, and my surroundings are such as I have never seen before in all my days.

I'm in a room with shiny gray shelves full of books, and waterlogged carpet surrounds me.

Running footsteps sound from between the shelves, then the gasp of a woman. And a choked splash as the book in her hand drops to the floor.

CHAPTER 3

Tress

A mountain of a man, drenched to the skin and scowling, is standing in front of me.

The copy of *Jane Eyre* drops to the floor as my hand lifts to my mouth to muffle the scream tearing its way through my chest.

Water soaks into my shoes, and I look down to see that I'm somehow standing in a pool of it.

I return my attention to the man in front of me. He looks nothing like the patrons I usually see down here. In fact, he doesn't look like he belongs here at all.

His dark hair is long. Colored beads wrap around a slim braid framing the deep frown and high cheekbones of a face tanned almost to a bronze. His outfit is unusual too, reminiscent of what I've seen volunteers wear at the seaport museum.

We get the occasional person under the influence at

the library, but I would have noticed this man crossing the lobby.

I *so* would have noticed this man.

"Who are you?"

The question that should be coming from me instead comes from him, and the deep voice delivering it sends shivers down my back.

"I work here."

"Here?" His sun lightened brows form a vee between eyes that have not let me go for a second since I turned the corner.

"At the library."

Cold settles in my stomach. I do indeed work here, and water is soaking into the carpet under my feet, and worse, into the pages of the book I just dropped.

I tear my eyes away from the stranger and snatch the paperback up from the wet floor.

The rank smell of the book proves it's been thoroughly soaked in saltwater. I inspect it, but I can already tell I'll be filling out a damaged book slip.

I look up again to the eyes that I assume have been on me this whole time.

"Where did all the water come from?"

He watches me quietly, as if assessing a threat.

I'm not used to being scrutinized, and it takes effort not to squirm under his steady gaze.

I have no idea what he is about to tell me.

A burst pipe? No, this is salt water. And in the middle of the room, no less. Far from the pipes hiding beyond the drywall.

How could someone have carried in enough seawater to drench an adult and soak the wall-to-wall carpet? I look around for crates or buckets of some kind.

"I am not certain."

Speaking again, clearly having come to some conclusion about me, the stranger's eyes survey the mess around him.

His reply is unsettling.

I take a step back.

Can I outrun him? I only need to make it to the stairway and up the two flights to the main floor.

He doesn't look drunk or high to me, but how does a grown man not notice how he got soaked in seawater? And more to the point, how on earth did he get in here without leaving wet tracks behind him?

The only entrances to the library are on the main floor.

Remembering the basement bathrooms, I pause. Maybe he got soaked in there?

Still eyeing him I retreat another step. Away from him.

"Excuse me, I need to..." I curse the tremble in my voice as I turn, charting the fastest course out of this situation.

"Stop."

The word is a command. One I know I shouldn't obey.

"Miss, please." His voice loses some of the rasp.

I turn, but my body feels like a coiled spring. I'm a fast runner. But faster than him? I don't know.

He takes a step towards me, and I shrink back. Retreating, he holds out a hand as if to still me.

"My apologies, miss." He clears his throat. "You say this is a library?"

I can't place his accent, but it can't be local.

I glance toward the stairs. I could have been up the first flight already. But I'm not entirely sure I can outrun this man, so I stay.

"Yes, sir. The public library."

He frowns as if the phrase is foreign to him, then he nods.

"Thank you."

"Um…" I hesitate before pointing him in the direction of the men's room, incidentally also away from the stairway.

"There are hand dryers in the restroom. They might help a little."

He bows his head. "I thank you, miss."

I swallow, and nod.

His leather boots squish with every step as he turns around, and he leaves large wet footprints in the carpet for the first few feet.

As the door closes behind him, I turn the corner at a jog. I consider leaving the return cart behind, but wanting to avoid another trip down here, I hurry over to grab it.

I pull the cart into the safety of the elevators and push the button.

As the doors close, I take my first full breath since dropping poor *Jane Eyre*.

"Someone spilled water in the basement?"

Chris uses a finger to push her cateye glasses further up her nose.

"Yes, there was a really wet guy, and a large stain of water surrounding him."

I don't mention the fact that it was undoubtedly salt water, or that he didn't seem to know where it came from.

My shoes are already showing the telltale white stains of drying salt. I'm going to have to soak them when I come home to keep the stains from setting.

"Was he intoxicated?"

"Not that I could tell. I think he's still in the men's room downstairs."

Her gaze drops to the book in my hand. "You dropped it in the water?"

"I was startled."

Her eyebrows rise, but she doesn't say what's obviously on her mind. But she also didn't walk into a soaked and scowling pirate in the basement.

"You know how to fill out a damage slip, right?"

"Yes."

She nods approvingly. "I'll call maintenance about the spill."

I take another breath of relief. Chris may be the closest thing I have to a friend, but she's also my boss. The line between supervisor and friend can't be easy to toe, but she does it masterfully.

The reprimand I deserve never passes her lips. Not for leaving patrons in the lobby, not for damaging library property.

And as I click through the order of a new copy of *Jane Eyre*, I am so grateful.

I don't see the stranger again until the next day, right before the close of my shift. This time he's considerably drier and, as we're in the main lobby surrounded by patrons and staff, a lot less unnerving. Still dressed in the same odd clothes as yesterday, he seems oblivious to the stares and whispers that follow him.

He leans over the counter towards me, but it's not uncomfortable.

The scent of sea water still wafts off him, as if he's recently taken a dip in the ocean.

"Miss? Have you any books on...magic?"

He drops to a whisper on the last word, as if the notion alone makes him uncomfortable.

"Fantasy books?"

"Aye?"

I have a feeling that the high fantasy we stock for readers of all ages isn't what he's looking for, but I get up from my chair and walk him over to the appropriate section.

I gesture to the computer on the table in the main aisle.

"If you are looking for a specific book title or author you can search here."

His eyes move from the computer to me, and he dips his head.

"Thank ye, miss."

I smile politely and walk back to my desk, but my head spins with questions.

Who is this man?

Where did he come from, and why is he dressed like a museum volunteer?

How did he manage to bring all the seawater inside the building?

The maintenance guy had been as clueless as I was as to how anyone could have deposited that amount of saltwater in the basement, but probably having faced more than a few unexplainable situations over the years he hadn't pressed me for a theory.

And I wouldn't have had one.

We get some strange types at the library. We're open to the public every day of the week, and unless someone is exceedingly smelly or disorderly, we don't censor our patrons.

I fiddle with the stapler on the desk as I fight the impulse to stare at the man I can't figure out.

I'm not the type to get carried away at the sight of a handsome face, but something draws me to this one.

We've never met before, I'm sure of that. And still, as fear clamped over my heart down in the basement, some other instinct had burst to life.

As if this man was already familiar to me.

Does he look like Eon?

But no, that isn't it. My brother is tall, but his shoulders aren't this broad and his skin could never tan to the deep bronze of this man's face and hands.

"What are you still doing here, Tress?"

Chris of the red cateye glasses, pokes her gray pixie cut over the counter to peer at me. Her perfume, like lavender and warm pies lingers in the air.

I turn to look at the large clock on the wall, and my eyes widen.

My shift ended half an hour ago. I've spent a good thirty minutes deep in thought about the man who is probably still browsing the Young Adult Fantasy section.

"Yikes. I guess I forgot the time."

Chris's red lips curve in a smile. "Anyone I should know about?"

My cheeks heat, despite her wrong assumption. I shake my head.

"Not at all."

She sighs, a look of disappointment on her kind face.

"I guess a woman can hope."

"Don't put too much stock in that hope."

Chris has known me for most of my life, better since I walked in asking for a job here in my junior year of high-school. Well enough that I don't need to explain my aversion to relationships. She may think, like others before her, that I'll change my mind. But I won't.

I'm so very done with love.

"I'll see you in the morning."

I grab my book bag and cross the lobby. The still warm August evening envelopes me as the heavy door slides shut behind me.

I make my way down the street and across the double crosswalk. I smile at an older man crossing to the side-walk behind me. He dips his head, eyes crinkling at the corners.

A family stands by a display window, discussing the treasures inside the shop. Their accents and clothes make it clear they're tourists, but they're dressed nothing like the man I left behind in the library's Fantasy section.

Something about his presence in the library seems unnatural, and I can't put my finger on it. Maybe he's just one of those people who enjoy dressing up in historical garb?

My mind stays on the strange encounter until my mind is jolted away from him by the sound of my labored breathing as I walk up the hill to my house.

I need to get into better shape.

This hill isn't exactly steep, and though my bag holds several checked-out volumes, it isn't what you'd call heavy.

I lug it onto the porch and unlock the door. Smells of home envelop me as soon as I step inside, but it's the scent of seawater that consumes my mind.

Or rather, the man that filled the basement air with it.

What was that crash I heard, really? How did a man like that walk right past my desk without me ever noticing? And why can't I stop thinking about him?

I flip the switch of the water kettle and stay lost in thought until the water is boiling. I probably should eat, but all I feel like doing is curling up on the couch with my cup of tea and my loot of books. And more, maybe that will get the man's piercing eyes off my mind.

After all, it's not like I'm interested in any way that counts.

Chris may think that all I need to reconsider my stance on relationships is the right man, but she's wrong.

They're all wrong.

For me, there's no such thing as a right man.

CHAPTER 4

Tress

Rocky Beach," Eon called this place where oddly shaped rocks cover the slope down to the ocean.

I drop down on one of them, and immediately the chill from the stone seeps through my skirt and tights.

Gray clouds hang low over an equally gray ocean. The air around me is pungent, and the cool salty breeze clings to my skin.

I've been coming to this beach since my parents let me roam unsupervised in our little seaside town, long before they ought to have.

Eon came with me the first few times when we were younger. On days with low tide we'd traverse the slippery rocks all the way out to Big Rock. On days with high tide we'd watch the tops of the biggest rocks from the small strip of dry sand left.

But it's been years since then. I no longer wear the hand-me-down overalls from my brother. I no longer stay shivering on the beach rather than going home to wait for the other shoe to drop.

I fold my arms around my knees, and rest my chin on my cotton tights. The weave is rough against my skin, and I breathe the calm I find only here.

It's been years, but still I watch the ocean and dream of a different life.

For both of us.

The man I saw soaked in the basement three days earlier has stood in front of the library's book-sale shelf for the last fifteen minutes.

It's not unusual for patrons to linger in that area, but usually they browse the books. This man seems to be staring specifically at the price chart over the books, as if waiting for new letters and numbers to jump out at him if he just gives it time.

I stand up from my chair and move around the desk to make my way over to him.

His presence at the library hasn't gone unnoticed in the last few days, and from what the rest of the staff has told me, I know he's been browsing the shelves from when the library opens in the morning until it closes at night.

He seems to be looking for something specific, but when asked he never wants help.

"Sir?"

He turns so fast I feel dizzy, and his gray eyes shoot to mine.

There's barely any space between us, not at all the professional distance I should be keeping.

I take a step away.

He levels me with an intense look that should be nerve-wracking, but for whatever reason, it doesn't repel me.

"Do you have any questions about the pricing list?"

I paste on my patented librarian smile.

His glance flicks to the pricing list for a moment as understanding dawns on his face.

"These are books that are for sale?"

I nod, as the pieces click in my mind.

"Do you not know how to read?"

The question blurts out before my brain has time to fully form the thought.

My face burns and I can't look at him.

It's the rudest way I've asked a question in my life.

"I apologize... I didn't mean to be rude."

"Apology accepted. And I do not."

I try to school my features this time, but my chin still drops at his admission.

Something flickers in his eyes, a decision?

"Miss? May I ask you to teach me?"

I'm still gaping.

"Teach you to read?"

"Aye miss. I have no coin, but if you need labor, I'll pay you with my back."

I try to hide my shock. From the look on his face, I don't think I'm doing it well.

How did this man reach his mid-thirties without at least a preliminary grasp on letters? A first grader could have read the sign above the books he clearly couldn't.

I had taken his artistic costume to mean he was an avid history enthusiast. But how likely is that if he doesn't read?

Did he once know, and later lose the ability? Through brain injury? Or substance abuse?

The last thought knots my stomach.

I should stay far away from this man. And not only because I don't have the first clue about teaching someone to read.

I've been a strong reader since Eon taught me before I started kindergarten, but if you were to hand me a test on phonics, I'm pretty sure I'd fail it outright. And grammar? Forget it.

"I'm afraid I don't—"

"You are literate, yes?"

"Um...yes? But I don't..."

"I don't expect your work for free, miss. I have no coin now, but as soon as I do, it's yours."

It's such a simple offer. So oddly phrased. It's one I shouldn't entertain.

I have a job, I have books to read. I know less than nothing about the eccentric stranger in front of me.

The gray eyes that watch me so intently look out of place in the calm, civilized setting we're in.

I note the slight freckles across his nose, the bronzed and weathered skin of his face and hands.

He looks like men I've seen in documentaries crossing oceans on rafts, proving history and discovering new continents. This man has an adventurer's soul, a free spirit made to roam. He was born to stand at the helm of a ship, sea spray in his face, and a wicked grin tilting his full lips.

I take a step back, trying to clear my head of the headiness of his presence, of the strong scent of bay rum and adventure clinging to the air around him.

What sort of situation is he caught up in? Do I even want to find out?

His eyes tip the scales.

I was betrayed by Jonah and abandoned by Luke, and the steadiness in these depths isn't something I can resist.

Stormy, like whipped seawater and steel gray clouds, his eyes speak to my heart.

Whatever his version of reality, he believes it fully.

"Miss?"

"I'm Tress."

I reach out my hand.

"Captain Charles William Seewell."

He takes my fingers in his, bends forward, and presses his lips to my knuckles.

My skin sparks with the contact.

"My pleasure, Mistress Tress."

I love my name on his lips.

What would he think of my full name?

"When?"

A laugh slips out of me at his eagerness, and I bite my bottom lip.

"You've got no time to lose, huh?"

His head dips at my comment, and though the request seems serious enough, humor flickers in his eyes.

My only plan after work is a date with a book.

My plans after work are always a date with a book.

"I could meet you in the Reading Room after work? I'll be done in another hour."

"Thank you, Miss Tress, I'm much obliged to you."

"Um, sure."

I turn to see a patron at the desk. Thankful for the distraction, I cross the room and slip behind the counter to help the young girl with a stack of books in front of her.

But even as I scan her card and notify her of the balance, I feel his eyes on me.

He doesn't strike me as a creep, but I'm not used to holding someone's attention like this.

Least of all a man who makes my mouth go dry.

And I've agreed to meet him after work. My heart speeds up at the thought, and I lift my eyes to search for him between the shelves of DVDs flanking the left side of the lobby.

He's not looking at me, but rather at the books on the shelves.

What is he looking for when he can't read?

I'm still staring when his eyes meet mine. He's too far away for me to decipher the look in them, but the way they hold mine makes my skin tingle.

My cheeks burn, and I drop my gaze.

What have I gotten myself into?

CHAPTER 5

Charles

If this place is hell, like I first thought, it's nothing like what I've been told. And if the woman I first laid eyes on in this place is a goddess of the underworld, here to tempt me to stay?

She might succeed.

Dark hair brushes across her shoulders with her movements as she slides behind the large desk in the front room of the building. Her voice is low and pleasant as she speaks to the woman standing on the other side of the desk.

Pink, like the sweetbriars growing by the ocean, blooms in her cheeks when she smiles. Is her skin as soft as the petals it resembles?

If she feels my gaze on her, she pays it no mind, instead she stares intently at the thin, black box standing upright in front of her.

The first woman leaves and another townsperson takes her place.

Tress exchanges stacks of books for nothing but pieces of paper, but the purpose of the transactions she handles isn't clear.

It's far from the only thing that eludes me about this place.

For three days I've spent my days at the library, my nights in a grove on the grounds behind it.

My first day here I saw a child, dressed as peculiarly as the adults with it, drinking water from a fountain inside the library. This one also public, and so I've not gone thirsty. The pastry the shopkeeper inside the library handed me yesterday was not enough to fill me, but it is far from the longest I've gone without food.

Hunger led me aboard the first ship I sailed, and it might lead me to another form of employment here.

Unless I find the book that has the power to bring me home.

I turn back to my search. My fingers glide between the books in the basket at my side, but none are bound in leather like the book I seek.

If I could trust this woman, Tress, with my plans to reunite with my ship and crew, I'd ask for her help.

But I know too little about how this place views what is clearly dark magic. It's not a chance I can take.

It's the same reason I have deflected the questions of the strangers approaching me about my clothes, common enough in the River Colony, but foreign to this town.

I move to the white shelves across the room, where hard boxes that aren't books, but thick pictures, line the walls.

There's no doubt this is a library, but it's like no library I have ever seen. Absent is the musty smell of leather and ink. The numerous books in these rooms are painted with vibrant colors. The covers are thicker than leather, and wrapped in a glossy material.

The doorways are high. The panes of glass so clear it's like they aren't there at all.

Merchant Monroe's substantial library was smaller than a quarter of this room, lit by candles, and the light from only a few windows. Every one of his books bound in leather in shades of earth.

And only his most important guests were invited in.

In my days here, I have seen men, women, and children walk freely in and out all day. I hadn't fully believed it at first, but it's clear it must be a library open to the public like the woman told me.

46

And somewhere in this building is the book that can give me my freedom.

I move further between the shelves until they open into a large space with chairs and tables along the edges.

In the middle of the space sits a large wooden base with a miniature barque mounted on top.

Three masts with full sails folding out from the yardarms. Ropes and chains straining as if pulled by a strong wind.

She looks as lifelike as if she might any moment escape the confines of this building, point her forecastle out towards the open sea, and sail out across the deep.

Does this place have more magic than I first thought?

Is the magic inherent in the building? And is that how I came to be here?

I move away from the barque and back towards the circular desk where the woman who calls herself Tress is still making her odd transactions.

I browse the shelf in front of me, but no leather book is to be found.

When I turn again to watch her, I find her eyes on me.

Her face pinks as she drops her gaze from mine, but I don't drop mine.

I hadn't planned to ask this woman to teach me to read. But as she eyed me, much longer than polite, the question made its way up my throat.

I expect that once I find it, the powerful book will require more than a simple touch to return me to my ship. I need to be certain I can decipher the inscriptions between the covers to find my way home.

Based on the skies outside this building, the sea is not far off. But as much as my soul aches to glimpse the waters I've called home for fifteen years, I haven't gone in search of them.

I need to find the book that can bring my vessel back to me.

A gray-haired woman dressed in mourning clothes takes Tress's place behind the counter, and before I know it the woman with cheeks like sweetbriars stands before me.

The soft smile on her face is sweet and innocent. Like that of the woman that betrayed me.

"Hi. Do you still want to work on some reading?"

Her voice is uncertain, as if my hatred of Merchant Monroe's daughter is clear on my face.

I dip my head, hoping my face has turned pleasant.

"Um, okay, the Reading Room is right this way."

She gestures to the hallway by the front doors, and I follow her.

My eyes are drawn to the peculiar garments showing off her full figure—tight stockings and short breeches, a shirt so tight it does nothing to hide the shape of her body underneath.

Nothing a woman would wear in the River Colony where I was born, nor have I seen such dress in any of the numerous ports I've visited.

Of all the females I've seen today, only two have worn anything resembling a dress. And their short skirts left little doubt of eschewed petticoats.

Tress turns to me as we walk through a second doorway to a room with a cold hearth.

"Is this good?"

I dip my head and lower into the seat across from hers.

Unbidden, memories crowd my mind. Of another woman who once promised to introduce me to the art of reading. When I'd made enough to live on from my plundering.

"We'll settle on land with my father's blessing, and I'll teach you. In our own parlor."

It wasn't the only promise she broke. Had she even then planned to abandon me for the blacksmith's son?

"Are you alright?"

The soft words pull me back to this room, as far away from my home as I've ever been.

But the woman across from me is just my tutor. It's all she, or any other woman, will ever be.

Tress's blue eyes are as innocent as Sarah's once were, full of hidden questions I want to answer.

Unfortunately for her, I know better this time.

CHAPTER 6

Tress

I've firmly entrenched myself in the staff gossip with my decision to help the sea captain learn to read.

My coworkers have apparently been dying for me to display some semblance of a love life. And spending one on one time with the mysterious man they've all been watching for days, qualifies.

I'd vented my frustrations to Chris earlier.

"I'm pretty sure I haven't expressed any romantic interest!"

She had pushed her red glasses higher up on her nose and winked at me.

"But it has not gone unnoticed that this devilishly handsome man seems quite taken with you."

I'd blushed, but even now, with my eyes trained on one of the several learning resources spread out between us, I feel his scrutiny on me.

Still, I don't agree with her assessment. The way he watches me doesn't feel like romantic interest. Charles Seewell studies me as if I'm a puzzle he can't solve.

It's my third afternoon in the Reading Room this week.

"Can you sound out this word?"

I'm clueless about teaching an adult to read, but after a phone call to the town's human services department, there are no local classes happening until early October, so I've resorted to help as best as I can.

He reads the word haltingly off the page.

"How about this one?"

I move a sparkling fingernail down the page to the picture of a ruler.

His large hand, sinewy and tan, follows mine.

My eyes linger on the thick gold band encircling the middle finger of his left hand, and the two thinner, ornate silver rings that wrap around his pointer and pinky.

Are these rings significant? Was he married once? Is he still?

I chide myself for the thought even as my gaze drops to his lips.

His mouth shapes the syllables, once, twice, before he tries to pronounce them together. Perfectly.

My gaze flits away from his mouth, meeting his eyes. When a grin breaks out on his stubbled face, I return it.

The light in his eyes makes my heart tilt a little bit.

But only because I enjoy his company—like anyone would.

I can spend my afternoons at the library across from a handsome man who smells of sea water and bay rum without repercussions.

Watching his lips as he sounds out two-syllable words isn't a surefire way to risk my heart.

This man is only a temporary distraction from the five years of lonely nights.

Like a new book, I will be able to close the covers when he moves on.

And he will move on.

They always do.

Good things always come to an end. No matter how much I want people to stay, they move on.

And leave me behind.

Even Jonah, who convinced me that he'd keep me safe, only to forget his promises at the first opportunity.

A blonde, long-legged opportunity.

Stories have kept me alive for a reason. All these years, stories have been my companions when I was left again and again.

Some people might read for pleasure, but I read for survival.

I spend hours in a world where Mr. Rochester's nutty wife sets fire to his bed, happily forgetting the difference between the life I thought I'd lead at thirty, and the life that is mine.

I close my tattered copy of *Jane Eyre* at the end of the day, and sleep soundly without screams from the attic, or fear of pyromaniacs in my bedroom.

A gasp of laughter filters out from between the bookshelves across the room.

Charles lifts his head, but doesn't comment.

Muffled giggles between the bookshelves are among my favorite things about the library.

But they are also a stark reminder of everything that ends when I close my book. The fellowship of friends, merriment of feasts, the music of fauns and dance of dryads.

The home I always longed for.

The dark-headed children and the husband I thought I'd have by now but don't.

I press my fingers against my breastbone, as if my touch can rub away the ache.

Charles eyes the movement and I drop my hand as if burned.

"How about this word?"

But my words are thin from embarrassment.

He sounds it out.

And I manage to keep my hands from covering my pink face.

The man across from me called himself captain, and he looks just like I'd expect a story book captain to look like.

His skin is the deep color of hours under the sun, of rays reflecting off the deep blue waters and burning his skin.

He even walks as if he expects the ground to shift. As if his norm is moving deck planks under his boots.

I've seen no one else with him. He's always alone.

Is he as lonely as I am?

Charles Seewell holds open the main door to the library, and I walk through it, into the cool evening.

Chris eyes us with unbridled curiosity. Her wink suggests the opinion she voiced earlier hasn't changed.

Keys rattle as she locks up, and I turn to the man I've spent the past two hours with.

"Have a good night."

He bows his head.

"Good night, Mistress Tress."

His long steps carry him down the ramp and he turns the corner.

Chris's heeled boots clack on the stone steps, and I follow her down the stairs.

"When are you doing your cozy little reading class next?"

She says it as if we do more than reading.

I roll my eyes.

"Tomorrow night?"

"And are there any sparks, yet?"

"No sparks."

In reality there are plenty, just none I'd ever act on.

A frown appears on her face.

"You're not lonely? You don't want to waste a perfectly good life, Tress."

Chris knows what she's talking about, I suppose. She met and married her husband at forty, and twenty years later he still kisses her across the library counter whenever he drops off her lunch.

"I'm not too lonely."

I know enough about loneliness to write a dissertation on it.

It doesn't mean I'm willing to trade it for a new relationship. It might ease the bone-deep loneliness for a bit.

But I've learned my lesson. From Lucas and Jonah—even my parents. Easing the loneliness only makes it come back like a hurricane.

And no man—no amount of sweet words or tender kisses—can ever be worth that raging return of solitude.

Chris sighs, then her eyes soften.

"Hmm, I think I know that look. Now tell me what you are reading tonight."

I purse my lips. "A Cinderella retelling space opera."

"I checked that one out to someone a few weeks ago. It looked good."

I pat my book bag where the book in question is waiting for me to walk the half mile to my house, put the kettle on, and curl up under a blanket.

Chris's little red Mini Cooper is parked by the curb. She drops her book bag on the passenger seat, and walks to the driver's side.

"Enjoy your book."

"Enjoy your husband."

Chris laughs at my retort, and winks at me.

"I'll tell John you said that."

I grin, knowing John will be nothing but flattered, and return her wave.

I trot across two crosswalks. My steps take me past the little yellow coffee shop that's supplied me with hot chocolate on many a winter walk.

Does Charles Seewell like hot chocolate?

I squash the thought down as soon as it appears. I might be making a jumble of teaching him to read, but we'll never have the kind of relationship that will include hot chocolate walks, or warm hugs...or anything else.

I close my eyes in hopes of shutting out my thoughts.

"Whoa there!"

My eyes snap open as a white-haired gentleman's hands lands on my shoulders, to avoid me running head-first into him.

I stagger back, mortification filling my chest.

"Oh my goodness! I'm so sorry."

"No worries, hon."

He chuckles at what I'm sure is a very vivid blush on my face.

I keep my eyes open as I pass the ice cream parlor. Tourists are still milling about, and will be for hours. This little town doesn't slow down until well after dark during the tourist season.

I pass the restaurant under the bridge, and keep my eyes looking straight ahead as I walk past the still-filled yellow outdoor tables.

I step across another double crosswalk and let my thoughts drift again.

I may have always wanted what Chris has, but it doesn't mean I'm not happily sequestered behind my shield of ink and paper.

I climb the hill too fast, and I'm heaving for breath as I reach my porch. I turn the key in the lock and step through the doorway.

I shut it behind me, and I'm alone.

My bookbag lands on my couch, my shoes in a pile by the door.

Minutes later a cup of tea is steaming on the coffee table and I'm turning the first page of my new conquest.

A real-life love story is not for me.

The love and companionship I find between the pages of my books is all I need.

All I want.

CHAPTER 7

Tress

In some ways both my brother and I made a living off our drug of choice.

I surrounded myself with the stories I clung to then—orchestrated a whole life within the pages of what was supposed to be entertainment.

Eon surrendered his life to the alcohol he leaned on years before my parents kicked him out at eighteen, and he used his savings for a bus ticket down to the city.

The wild roses that grow between the rocks on Rocky Beach are gone. Every silky, pink petal has fallen to the sand, leaving behind green bushes ripe with deep orange rose hips.

I lean forward from my perch on the rock and let my fingers slide along the bulging fruits. One comes off in my hand.

I bite into it. The slightly sour, earthy flavor on my tongue reminds me of long ago days when Eon and I used to pick them for tea.

They are the first sign of fall, of cooling temperatures, and soon-to-be white-frosted mornings.

Dread curdles in my stomach at the thought of the freezing nights my brother will soon face.

He calls me sometimes, when he's able to borrow a phone, but even when he won't admit it, I know he sleeps more often on the streets than at the shelter.

It's not something a little sister can easily stomach.

I hear the scuffle before I see it. The darkness is only penetrated by the yellow light of the wall lights lining the closed doors of the library.

I tug the keys out of the lock and drop them into my pocket where they jingle as I'm drawn towards the voices.

They sound as if they're just around the corner.

Without thinking, I bypass the stairs and the way home and start down the ramp that winds around to the back of the building.

Neither the brush of greenery against my hand nor the quick sharp scent of the bushes inspires a return of my common sense.

Chasing voices in the dark isn't your best idea.

Still I press forward.

"No. I have not bothered anyone. I'm simply in search of a place to sleep."

The familiar voice tugs me closer until I'm upon them.

Two police officers, badges glinting in the light from lamp posts in the park behind the library, and a shadow of a man between them.

"Unhand me."

I'm too busy paying attention to the strange accent of the voice to decipher why the anger lacing it doesn't scare me, when it probably should.

"Stay back, miss."

The officer's voice is stern, and I almost listen.

The man he's towering over isn't Eon. But my heart pulls at me as if it is.

I step closer, and the warning sounds again.

"Miss, I need you to stand back!"

The man on the ground stands, hands away from his body, and in the soft light, I recognize the bronzed face that belongs to the voice.

Charles Seewell looks thunderous. The width of his shoulders and size of his hands tells me he could easily hurt these men if he wanted to. How, after attempting to cajole him over to their patrol car, are they still standing?

"Wait, I know him!"

The officer closest to me pauses his reach for something in his belt.

"You know this person? Is he staying with you?"

"Yes!"

The answer is out before my brain can alert me to what an impossibly bad idea this is. I don't know Charles Seewell anywhere near enough to invite him to stay with me.

But the looks I'm getting from the men in uniform do nothing to inspire me to take it back. They don't believe me.

And why should they?

I don't look like the kind of girl to keep company with the man now staring me down as if I have lost my mind.

And I might have.

"What is his name, miss?"

The closest officer, not much taller than me, but twice my weight in muscles, turns a suspicious glance my way.

"Charles Seewell. He's a friend of my brother's."

It's too much information, but the officers don't seem to care. Liars are notorious for adding more details than necessary, and I'm not a very good one.

The two men share a look, then as if making a decision, turn back to me.

Perhaps they'd rather he go home with me, than having to fine him for sleeping outside the library.

Is that what's going on?

"What's your name, Miss?"

"Treasure Hayden."

"And your address?"

I rattle it off, feeling Charles's eyes on me the whole time.

What does he think of this? Has he slept on the library grounds this whole week? Does he really have no place to go other than the streets of this little town?

As far as I know, we don't have much of a homeless situation around here, and I'd just assumed he'd come from somewhere and that he went back there whenever the library closed for the night.

Charles still hasn't spoken a word to me as the officers get back in their car.

This is a terrible idea.

I'm kicking myself for my impulsivity, but it's too late now.

Something beyond the reach of the warm lamp light scurries across the lawn and into the rhododendron bush that was to have been Charles's bedroom.

The thought that he's slept outside this week still overwhelms me. Suddenly I'm relieved the last couple of days have been dry.

"My house is this way."

I start walking, assuming he'll follow.

I hold on to the slight hope that he won't, except the officers are still watching us through the windshield of their patrol car.

Charles's footsteps sound behind me.

If I hadn't spent all day pushing away thoughts of winter coming and Eon sleeping on the streets, would I be in this situation now?

"I thank you, Miss Hayden."

Charles's long legs have no trouble keeping up with my fast pace as we round the library corner and move down the street.

"It's fine."

It isn't fine.

Every step down the sidewalk feels like a noose around my neck, and I can't even look at him.

My mind is running in a million directions at once to

find a way out of the predicament I've made for myself.

The streets are brightly lit with lamp posts and even a display window decked out in fairy lights. I stare at the display of driftwood and ocean themed pottery and wish I thought just a little better on my feet.

What should I do? How can I possibly solve this?

I smile at a couple pushing a stroller with a sleeping toddler. Another group of tourists stare at Charles's outfit, and I hear their whispers as we pass them.

The night air is warm and if this was any other night, I'd enjoy the walk. Tonight it's tainted by the fact that I've invited a virtual stranger to my home and implied I'll house him for the night.

The half mile back home is quickly eaten up by my hurried steps, and when we walk up the steps to my porch, together, I have no better idea of what to do than I did back at the library.

"Miss Hayden, I thank you for your hospitality."

"You're welcome."

But I can't meet his eyes as I say the words.

"I don't expect you to lodge me in your home. I'd be happy with an outbuilding."

I almost laugh, but there's nothing funny about this situation.

The small house I call home doesn't have any out-buildings, unless you count the trashcans sitting against the side of it.

"I'm afraid I don't have a ton of outbuildings."

"Right here is good."

He gestures to the porch floor.

The stranger I've accidentally picked up by trying to save him from a fine I'm sure he can't pay wants to sleep on my porch.

What do I do in a situation like this?

There's been nothing in my former experience to prepare me.

If he'd been my brother, that after all our years apart I'd honestly know about as well, I'd let him stay on my couch. But I have no shared childhood memories with Charles Seewell.

It doesn't sit well with me to have him sleep outside, but I can't bring myself to ask him inside.

John would have a conniption if I did.

A smile twitches on my lips at the mental image of Chris's steadfast husband having anything close to a fit of hysterics. But it doesn't help my current situation.

"You're a single woman living alone, Tress. You can't afford to be gullible."

John had been right to insist I take more precautions for my safety. But going for walks after dark isn't the same as inviting strangers for sleepovers. I'm not normally this stupid.

I wring my hands.

How do I approach this? If he's truly homeless, has he even had anything to eat today?

"I don't...um...would that be okay?"

"Mistress Hayden, I am not familiar with your justice system, but I believe you saved me from further trouble tonight, and I'd be happy with the ground."

His accent isn't the only foreign thing about him, the words he uses are too. His phrases are stilted and formal, almost archaic.

"Should I bring you some food?"

He shakes his head.

"I could give you a blanket?"

"I thank you for that."

When I come back out with one, he accepts it with a bow.

But even after the door is locked and I'm tucked under my down comforter with a cup of tea on my nightstand, I can't sleep.

Tonight's not a cold night, but it's not one I'd pick to sleep outside either.

My thoughts circle around the boy with the dimple in his right cheek, whose brown eyes saw too much when he was so young.

In my memories Eon's barely in middle school, shielding me from the angry hands meant to punish some childish act of mine.

The faraway look in his eyes as he steps onto the bus to get as far away as possible from everything he's ever known is branded onto the back of my eyelids. As if I just saw it in real life yesterday.

His voice that I barely recognized the last time he'd called me, resounds in my head, his words slurred and as far from sober as a man could be.

No, I can't sleep.

Not when a man who has been nothing but polite to me is sleeping on the plank floor outside my front door.

I jump out of bed, making sure my pajamas are decent, and tip-toe down the stairs and out to the porch.

He really is sleeping out here, my fuzzy throw covering his curled-up form. I bend down and touch his shoulder.

"Mr. Seewell?"

He's a captain, isn't he? Is it rude of me to refer to him as mister? Or is Captain Seewell just some sort of alter ego?

His eyes open, instantly alert and as piercing as ever.

Tension fills the air as he coils for a threat I'm not.

Recognition dawns in his eyes, and the tension fades.

"Mistress Hayden."

"You can call me Tress."

He sits up, and I straighten.

Why did I just give him permission to call me by my first name?

"Your full name is Treasure?"

Did he listen in as the officer took my name and address?

"It is."

"Treasure."

He says it again, as if trying it on for size.

My full name sounds every bit as delectable on his lips as I thought it might.

I push the thought away, knowing what a field day Chris would have with that information, if she knew.

His voice is rough with sleep.

My heart does a little flip it has no business doing.

Captain Seewell and I are strangers, not lovers, and my heart needs to get the memo.

"Do you need assistance, Treasure?"

My cheeks burn.

I haven't told him why I'm out here. For all he knows, I'm waking him up in the middle of the night to give him permission to use my first name.

I push the words out through a throat that is tight with anxiety. But I don't let it stop me.

"Please, come sleep in the front room. It's too cold out here."

He doesn't argue with me this time, but grabs my fuzzy blanket and follows me inside. Perhaps he really is cold.

I point to the couch in the front room, and he nods his head in thanks.

I leave him with a, "Goodnight," and then I sprint up the stairs and lock my bedroom door.

This time, I curl up under the covers and go right to sleep.

CHAPTER 8

Tress

"Treasure."

I can't get enough of the way he says my name, as if I am what I'm called.

We are strangers, but my name on his lips, his voice somehow both rough and melodious, makes me hope that one day I *will* be treasured. Before coffee, it makes me a little dizzy.

His presence on my couch on a Saturday morning makes my head spin too.

When he sits up, he fills the room in a way I couldn't have imagined.

It feels no more normal than when I first saw him, soaked in sea water, in the library basement a week ago.

My heart stutters to life.

"Do you have time for some coffee?"

He dips his head and the light catches on the gold ring in his ear. "I thank you, Treasure."

Sunlight dances across the dark planks of my living room as my bare toes step off the stairs and onto the cold floor.

His clothes are the only outfit I've ever seen him in, and now I understand why.

Does he even have access to food?

I walk into the kitchen to turn the kettle on. Minutes later I step back into the front room with two steaming cups of coffee.

"Cream?"

He shakes his head, and takes a cup.

"Thank you."

An easy quiet settles over the room as we both nurse our cups. Caffeine slowly seeps into my bloodstream as I steal glances at the man across from me.

Billowy shirtsleeves, wide pants tucked into leather boots. The burgundy sash under his belt.

He's dressed like a pirate.

All my theories about this man have been wrong. He's not a history enthusiast, a reader, or a volunteer. He doesn't even appear to have a home.

Maybe you need to stop assuming and go straight to the source?

I gulp down another sip of caffeine for courage and open my mouth.

"Can I ask where you're from? I mean, where do you live?"

"The Lady Monroe has been my home for the past five years."

His gaze on me is so intense I can't look away, his voice the kind that doesn't ask, but demands attention.

"Where were you born?"

"In the River Colony."

Cold settles in my stomach. I don't know where that is. Or where it *was*.

"In America?"

"The British Colonies, yes."

My mouth drops open and my head spins.

Am I nuts for having brought this stranger to my home?

I pour coffee down my throat, to hide my discomfort, then wheeze as the hot drink goes down my windpipe instead.

Charles is next to me in a second, his hand on my arm.

Scalding coffee burns my throat.

I choke and sputter as tears run down my cheeks.

"I'm sorry, I'm fine."

I cough the words, and hope I don't look as pathetic as I think I do.

I put my coffee cup down on the side table and escape to the bathroom off the hall.

I shut the door behind me, close my eyes and groan.

So smooth, Tress.

I wipe my face with a washcloth until my skin isn't quite as red and my eyes not quite as watery, before I return to the living room.

No more embarrassing coughing fits, please.

"Would you like some breakfast?"

The question surprises even me, but the sea captain in my living room accepts.

I leave him to his coffee while I whip up the batter and heat the pan.

One by one I drop rounds of soon-to-be pancakes into my cast iron pan. They sizzle as the surface grows less shiny, then bubbly, and I flip them with the golden side up.

The golden side might also be edged in black. Just a little.

"Here."

I hand him a stack of pancakes topped with a melting lump of butter and a generous drizzle of maple syrup.

Jonah used to call them "drowned in sugar."

But Jonah is not here.

I grab my own stacked plate and take my seat on the loveseat across from him. The way he inhales the food makes my heart smart.

Does Eon do this?

Eat as if the hunger is alive within him, threatening to consume him if he doesn't quench it?

Sweet, buttery, and fluffy as always, not even pancakes can quite hold my attention while sharing a space with this man.

Finally, Captain Seewell's fork clangs against his empty plate, and he leans back against the couch pillows.

He moves, as if to carry the dishes to the kitchen, but I couldn't care less about the dishes.

Instead, I ask the question that's been burning on my tongue since I walked downstairs this morning.

"Will you tell me more about yourself?"

His movements pause, and those eyes are back on me again, searching, as if he has reason to be hesitant to tell me more about himself.

Does he?

His eyes move to the mantelpiece that houses a scented candle and the only picture I still have of me and

Eon—standing on Rocky Beach, his arm slung over my shoulder, light still in his eyes.

Charles seems to mull my question over as his thumb and pointer finger wrap absentmindedly around his chin, dragging down as if he once used to stroke his beard the same way.

He clears his throat, and I ignore the tingling sensation across my skin at the sound.

"I began my life at sea as a cabin boy on the Blossom when I was just fifteen…"

Daylight streams through the windows into my living room. It highlights the dust in the air in dancing swirls, but I pay it no mind.

Because from the moment he opens his mouth, the story he tells me is captivating, thrilling, and…completely unbelievable.

His words can't possibly be true, but the more he tells me, the more I want to believe them.

I try to avert my eyes, but every syllable that falls from his lips makes it more impossible not to stare, or to soak up every word.

His voice is melodic and deep, and the effect it has on me is profound.

Eon and I swam in the ocean as kids, racing each other to the red buoy, clinging to the cold plastic, and shuddering whenever our feet touched the slimy chain attached to it.

I can still feel the pull of the waves on my limbs.

The story filling my living room puts a similar spell on me—I can no more resist it now than I could the pull of the ocean waves then.

The intensity in the sea captain's voice, in his eyes. It pulls me out—out. Pushes me in—in, back to shore.

I will never fall in love again, but this story, and the voice telling it, is the closest I've come to temptation.

"He's been sleeping in the park, Chris."

Should I really tell her this?

I'm not one hundred percent sure I should. Chris is my superior at work, and even if she wasn't, I'm worried she'll frown on my actions last night.

To be honest, even I am frowning on them.

But I have no one else to confide in.

"It's not technically illegal."

She pushes her glasses up on her nose and stares at her computer screen, but she's not fooling me—I have her attention.

"And I think the cops were about to arrest him, and—"

"For sleeping in the park? That can't be right. I'm fairly certain there's a law against that."

She straightens and the gaze that connects with mine is the kind I'm afraid can look straight through to my soul. It's the kind of gaze I always imagined mothers to have.

"What do you mean 'they were about to?' Did you stop them?"

I grab a book from the stack to my left and swipe it across the scanner on my desk—too fast, and I need to repeat the action.

Looking intently at the screen, I pretend I'm looking for the correct category to place it in.

My brain unhelpfully blends the words into each other.

"I might have…um, interrupted them? A little?"

"Tress!"

The annoyance in Chris's voice is real this time.

"Please don't tell me you let him stay at your place."

The screen in front of me blurs. I don't have a great defense for my actions.

Chris has known me all my life. She knows about Eon and where his choices have led him. She knows as well as I do that he probably spends nights in parks and on sidewalks.

But she isn't his sister.

That information can't possibly do to her what it does to me.

"I didn't! Well, not exactly, and—"

"Treasure Hayden, did you let a stranger stay in your house overnight? A *male* stranger?"

I scoff at her implication. "Yes, because only males can be criminals."

"A female would be less likely to have twelve inches and a good fifty pounds on you."

She has a point.

"Not to mention that the man looks like he's mostly muscle."

Again she isn't wrong. I have no doubt who would win in a scuffle between me and the man who slept on my couch last night. But I'm also certain he had no plans to hurt me.

I turn to her, completely abandoning my pretense of categorizing books.

"He stayed on my porch. At least to begin with. But then I couldn't sleep, and—"

Chris lets out a sound as if I just admitted to kicking a puppy.

"I went downstairs and asked him to sleep on the couch."

She groans, rests her elbows on the desk and presses her fingertips against her temples.

"Tress, you're going to die young if you keep this up. Do I need to have John talk to you again?"

It's not a real threat, but her retired police officer husband did have a talk to me about safety when he found out about my post-midnight weekend walks a few years ago.

"You don't have to worry John. I'm here, whole and hale, and I won't let it happen again."

"Uh-huh. And where is this gentleman sleeping to-night?"

"Not on my couch!"

The answer comes out too fast. Chris wasn't born yesterday, and her eyes bore into me.

"I haven't said anything, but I was going to let him stay, maybe, again tonight if I couldn't get a hold of the human services department, and…"

Chris picks up the phone and hands it to me, her red fingernail clicking against the laminated list of community phone numbers in front of me.

"Their number is listed in the directory right there. Call them."

She watches me as I make the call, abandoning whatever else the town pays her to do in favor of making sure I find a solution that doesn't involve anyone sleeping on my couch.

And I do.

It's easier than I think to find my overnight guest a place to stay. Despite the fact that I didn't even think we needed one, we do have a homeless shelter in my town—it's even within walking distance of the library.

Was that where the officers were taking him last night?

The feeling of relief that trickles through me isn't because I won't need to house a stranger tonight. It isn't even because Charles now has a place to sleep.

Charles Seewell is staying in town. If not forever, at least for now.

He will be able to keep coming to the library. To keep attending my painfully ineffective reading lessons.

I'll be able to listen to more of his stories of his years at sea told in a voice meant for storytelling.

My heart soars as I walk into the Reading Room when my shift is over, and I'm sure it's visible on my face.

My eyes settle on the broad shoulders that stretch his linen shirt, the one that looks a little more unkempt than it was days ago.

Do I only notice it now because I know he's been living on the streets?

But he won't have to anymore.

He'll get to sleep in a bed and have access to showers and food.

And I will be able to stay a little longer in this odd friendship that, for the first time since my brother left, makes me feel as if the aching loss won't consume me. Nothing can ever replace my brother, but this man fills places in my heart that have long been empty.

When Charles looks up at me from his seat at what I now think of as "our table," inexplicable joy spreads its warm waves throughout my chest, filling me, spilling over.

I want to hold on to the sense of adventure that clings to him like a second skin. I want to remember what it felt like to hang out with my brother, even if this man is nothing like him.

I want this friendship—more than I've wanted anything in a long time.

I laugh at the surprised look on his face.

But then the corners of his eyes crinkle, and his lips tilt with a half-smile.

"Will you tell me another story?"

My question is laced with expectation, with an eagerness I know I should tone down.

But that half-smile widens and a flash of teeth accompanies his answer.

"Would you like to hear one about the time we escaped a navy schooner outside of Charleston?"

"Yes, please."

I take a seat next to him as he launches into another story.

And this is not the last time I'll see him.

CHAPTER 9

Tress

The decision to pick up Anja's shift had been easy. I'd jumped at the chance to help the sea captain—if that is what he really is—with his reading skills and to listen to another one of his stories.

Stories that are beginning to trump the ones found on my bookshelves.

I'm at the edge of my seat across from him, nearly forgetting that I'm supposed to be helping him with phonics. Instead, I'm hanging on every word he speaks.

It's a thrilling tale made up of unfortunate word choices, prideful retaliation, and...a very large mountain of manure?

I hold my breath as Charles continues.

"We found Will hours later, covered in a pile of...well."

A smile plays at the corners of his mouth, the fondness for his friend clear.

I laugh. The story paints a rather vivid picture of Will, and one I'm glad I don't have to smell in real life.

"Is Will older or younger than you?"

Charles frowns as he thinks about this, rubbing a hand along his jaw. The cuff of his linen shirt makes a starker contrast to his skin than before, since the shelter apparently lets him launder his clothes. It's odd to get the occasional whiff of detergent off of him now.

"A year or so younger, I think?"

Will is a permanent feature in all of Charles's stories to the point that I almost feel like I know him. But I don't know Charles's reckless companion in his stories anymore than I know the man sitting across from me.

Out of the two of them, I know for a fact that the man in front of me is real. But is he who he says he is? And if he's not, who is he really?

We've spent a week like this, ever since the morning he woke up in my front room and told me that first story.

And as much as I've tried to keep from getting attached, every story he tells feels like it bridges the distance just a little.

The way his eyes light up in the middle of a tale, the shifting cadence of his voice—like music pulling at heartstrings. He pauses at the perfect moment, the one where everything hangs in the balance, and I'm hanging on his every word.

He's a born storyteller, and for a girl who has lived and breathed stories for so long, it's almost impossible to resist. But I will resist it, because I know what happens when I don't.

Heartbreak is what happens when you let yourself get carried away.

And I could see how I could. I can easily imagine what his touch might feel like, what it would feel like to earn the fondness in his smile when he speaks of the man who is like a brother to him.

But though his stories are fraught with danger and humor, usually at Will's expense, there is never…romance.

And it makes me wonder.

My eyes fall to the rings on his fingers. Do they have meaning? Is there a love story in his past? In his present?

I almost ask. But I clamp the question down instead.

I have no right to ask something so personal of him when he's not sharing it freely. I haven't shared anything that personal with him.

And I won't.

I won't make the mistakes I made with Lucas again. Not even for a man who seems to have jumped right out from one of my beloved stories.

We part ways at the library doors as usual. The homeless shelter where he now lives is just a couple of streets away.

I shove the key into the lock and twist until the mechanism clicks.

Then I turn to Charles.

His eyes are on me, and I think they might have been the whole time.

My mouth goes dry.

"Good night, Mistress Hayden."

His deep voice makes my stomach do a little tumble.

A completely unauthorized tumble.

I pretend as if I don't notice, even as my skin tingles.

"Goodnight...Captain Seewell."

He dips his head, and I turn away, eager to hide a blush.

I have no reason to blush. He's just a stranger. A stranger I've spent hours with each night over the last week and a half, but a stranger no less.

"You can come home with me. You don't have a boy-friend, right?"

The rough voice sends a shiver down my spine, but for all the wrong reasons.

The man who has followed me ever since I passed the bustling dive bar across the street from the ice cream shop, sidles closer. As if I've encouraged him in some way. And I haven't at all.

"No. I need to get home."

I've walked these same streets on my own at all hours of the night in the past, and I've never felt unsafe. But tonight I do, and I find myself wishing I wasn't here alone.

"You're so pretty, and I don't live far from here?"

I hope he means a hotel, because the thought that this creep lives in my town is terrifying.

But the rasping voice doesn't seem to understand that my repeated no's are rejections.

I don't know if he's drunk or stupid, or both. But he is relentless.

"No, I—"

"I've got money, is that what you want?"

He steps in front of me, pulling out his wallet for me to see.

I shrink back.

I need to walk back towards the library, back to where there's people.

Showing this guy where I live isn't a solution.

I would have gone back already, if I hadn't thought I'd lost him a block ago.

Why didn't I turn around as soon as I realized he was behind me? But I also just want to get home.

I speed up my steps until I leave him behind, still headed towards home.

If I run, can I make it home before he catches up with me?

"I've got fifties in here, you'd—"

His words break off on a pitiful squeak. A thud and a grunt of pain fills the air.

My heart pounds against my ribcage as I spin around.

A giant man towers over my unwelcome companion. He snarls, and pushes the smaller man up against the brick wall of the building next to us.

The yellow light of a street lamp up the street glints off what can only be a knife blade held against my stalker's neck.

I can't stop the shriek that tears up my throat.

The man with the knife looks over his shoulder at me, and terror courses through me. It throbs through my limbs as breath catches in my throat.

I need to run.

I need to hide, to get away.

But my feet are frozen to the ground.

I can't move. Can't breathe. Can't...

"Mistress Hayden, are you unharmed?"

The attacker is Charles Seewell.

The thought rushes in with relief, but it can't quite dispel the terror gripping me.

It's only Charles.

Even if I can't see him clearly in the shadows of this part of the street, I know him.

He won't harm me.

And still the adrenaline coursing through me takes my voice.

He takes a step closer to me, dropping the knife against the throat of the creep who's been pressed against the brick wall. He drops to the ground, and I shudder as I look at him first, then at Charles.

"Did you...kill him?"

My question is half gasp, half squeak, and I don't want an answer.

Charles grunts, shakes his head, and kicks the man on the ground.

The man lets out a groan and crawls to the corner. He gets to his feet and glances back at Charles and me with terror in his eyes.

Charles takes a menacing step towards him, and the man who propositioned me disappears down the side-street at a waddling run.

How badly did Charles hurt him?

Charles's hand is on my arm, drawing my attention back to him.

"Are you hurt?"

His voice is gruff.

I pull in a shaky breath, trying to calm down, but I can't stop the tears coursing down my cheeks.

I'm not hurt physically, but my throat refuses to let the words out.

I shake my head.

He sheaths his knife and looks at me as if he doesn't know what to do next.

But I do.

We need to get out of here.

If the man he attacks finds one of the numerous po-lice cars crawling around town tonight, and tells his story, Charles will be in hot water.

And this time I won't be able to talk him out of it.

"We need to go."

I grab his hand and pull him with me. As if I could ever pull this giant of a man anywhere without his full cooperation.

But, hand clamped over mine, he follows me the last block to my house.

I take the steps to my front porch two at a time, and he follows without problem.

I let go of his arm and force my shaking fingers to dig in my purse for the keys and to unlock the door.

My hands are slick, and the keys slip out of my grip.

I stoop to pick them up and try again.

The keys clatter to the porch floor boards.

Terror speeds in my chest.

I need to get him out of sight!

"I can't get the door open, and if the cops listen to him, I don't know how to help you, I—"

My words break off on a sob.

Charles's warm fingers close around mine.

"Let me."

He slips the keys from my sweaty grip to his calloused fingers.

The lock clicks, and the door swings open.

I grab his arm and pull him inside the house with me.

Once inside, I lean my back against the closed door, panting as if I've been running this whole time.

In some ways I have.

I don't even care that I've left the keys in the outside lock. They can stay.

"Treasure."

I'm shaking so violently I'm worried I'll fall. And my words that before were not to be found tumbles out of my mouth as if they'll never stop.

"You could have gotten arrested, he could have... You could have hurt him. He could have..."

My rambling words trail off as he pulls me into his arms.

I stiffen, but he does nothing but embrace me. His strong arms around me ask for nothing, and his words are gentle, patient. Concerned.

"Are you hurt, Treasure?"

I shake my head, overwhelmed tears making their way back up until words are unable to pass the lump in my throat.

His arms tighten around me, and the tears return full force.

I sob into his shirt.

His voice rumbles through his chest, and his breath warms the top of my head.

"Shh, I'm sorry I scared you. I wanted to make sure you arrived home safely and saw him follow you, heard his suggestion, and I..."

His grunt finishes the sentence. His grip on me tightens, and he rests his chin on my head.

I shouldn't welcome this contact, should I?

He's still a stranger.

But his embrace feels so right. Too right.

I press closer, inhaling the faint smell of the ocean that still lingers on his clothes, on his skin.

His arms feel nothing like what I thought they would. I promised myself I would never be in this position again, never let another man put his arms around me again.

But now that I am, and he is, I don't want it to end.

I don't know how he got here, or how he's come to mean so much to me in such a short time.

His arms shouldn't feel like safety, but they do.

And that should scare me.

Safety has never been a lasting thing in my life, and this man won't be different.

But my heart beats faster.

Not in fear.

It doesn't listen.

Instead it sighs deeply, as if it has just come...

Home.

CHAPTER 10

Charles

I loved a woman once. Fell for her innocent eyes and soft words, tangled in her web of lies until I changed my future.

For her.

But a man would be hard pressed to make a mistake like that twice.

As I spin my tale in the library's reading room on a Sunday morning, bright sunlight weaves through the clear window panes and Treasure's excitement fills the air.

Her hesitation to meet my eyes this morning made me wonder if perhaps I overstepped last night.

"Thank you for last night. That was a good thing you did."

"You're welcome."

She stepped back then, as if worried I'd embrace her again.

She has nothing to worry about.

It's been a long time since I let merchant Monroe's daughter's guileless eyes inspire me to a loyalty she never returned. Since I let her faithful promise push me to work harder and longer to give her the home she deserved.

Instead she found someone else to give her what she wanted. My sacrifices forgotten before I was even out of port.

I learned my lesson standing by her grave, the knowledge that the child that took her wasn't of me clawing at my chest.

Women may be the fairer sex, but they have no less guile than men. So I have no loyalty to give a woman.

Even when tempted with wide blue eyes that pull on every thread of desire I've ever felt.

Treasure Hayden is perched at the edge of the stuffed chair, as if she's ready to leap out of her seat and into the tale I've been weaving for the past hour.

Last night she cried, trembled, in my arms, but in this moment her eyes are clear and her face flushed with life.

The reservation from this morning is nowhere to be seen as she meets my eyes, her own full of sparkle as she hangs onto my every word.

I clear my throat, unable to drag my eyes from the mix of excitement and horror on her face. This story does not end well for me.

"The air was still thick with heat, and although I'd taken my time to get to the docks to avoid suspicion, it didn't take me long to get back.

I could already see the ship and my crewmen at the dock when the man I'd argued with earlier stepped around the corner."

The noise of pity Treasure makes fills the room and almost derails my story.

"Before I had a chance to move to defend myself a thick, hairy arm crushed against my windpipe. And as the hits rained down on me, I saw his smirking face watching me go down from a safe distance."

I water down the details of the ambush outside a bar in Newport, and still her eyes widen.

"They beat me bloody and left me for dead in that alley."

Her pink lips part, and she lets out a gasp that tightens my gut.

"What happened after? Did your crewmen find you?"

"I don't know exactly what happened. I woke seven days later in the guestroom of a merchant's house."

I'd opened my eyes and looked straight into the deceptively innocent gaze of Sarah Monroe.

But I leave that out.

Miss Hayden and I will never have that intimate of knowledge of each other.

Our pasts, or hearts, need not be fully known by the other.

That is, if there is still a heart that beats in this old pirate's chest. Perhaps it is something else by now. Something blackened, warped.

Dead.

"Are you okay? What's wrong?"

Treasure's voice is soft with concern, her normally smooth brow furrowed.

How does she read the changes in my mood so easily?

I shake my head and tilt my lips for her benefit.

She doesn't need to know the darkness I carry as my constant companion.

Treasure scoots back into her chair, as if just now realizing how close she's been to tipping off her seat entirely.

The moments of my past have come back to life in this room, and her expressive face has entertained me more than the telling of my tale.

A small smile dances along the line of her mouth, tilting the corners.

"This is what it feels like, you know."

"This?"

I frown, unsure of her implication.

"Reading. The stories I read? They make me feel just like this. You are a very skilled storyteller, Captain Seewell."

"I find it hard to believe that the markings in a printed book can replace a told tale."

"But oh, they can, Charles. You'll see!"

I'm startled by her use of my given name. She's given me permission to use hers, but she's never before used mine.

Her lips continue moving as she speaks about her love for the written word, but I can't make out the words for the thoughts crowding my mind. They're like fish gathered in a net about to be hauled over a railing—silvery, slippery, constantly moving.

I don't know the story she's just told me, but I do know that I want to watch her face when she reads her books.

Will I see it change with every word as I've seen today?

Can her written books possibly equal the magic of a well-spun story?

When I walk into the library the next morning, I find her curled up on the leather couch in that same room, and I have my answer.

She told me yesterday she didn't work today, and I don't know why she's here when she has comfortable housing nearby, but I am thankful she prefers this place.

Because here I can watch her undisturbed. I let my eyes roam over the scene in front of me.

The cover of the book in her hand is the color of tropical waters. Between her slender hands I glimpse a stack of books, and atop it, a style of lamp I've seen in use in ports far from home.

It's one of her modern books, nothing like the Monroes' leather bound volumes. These pages are bound in an impossibly thin cover of thick, painted paper.

But the book itself holds my attention only for a second.

Treasure's face, the light in her eyes and quirk of her lips, has me mesmerized.

The quick dart of her tongue, the widening of her eyes as she turns the page both hold my attention as if by magic.

Her face changes while her eyes track the inked letters of the pages, and something shifts in my chest.

Imperceptible, if not for the slash of terror that follows it.

I swore I would never fall for another set of guileless eyes, and I have not.

Since the day I stood on the soil into which Sarah's body had been lowered, knuckles still smarting from the bearded jaw of her widower, I have not strayed from my resolve.

A blackened heart like mine cannot beat back to life again. Not after all these years.

But even as I deny the thought, fear fills me.

I fear my denial comes too late for my worn heart.

That this woman, named for gems and gold, holds it in her hands already.

CHAPTER 11

Tress

I'm lost in the inked letters that dot the page.

My body is curled up on the leather loveseat by the fireplace in the library, but my mind sneaks through a library where I should not enter, to steal books I'm not allowed to read.

My heart knocks against my ribcage as a man just a few years older than me makes me wonder how people fall in love.

I don't tell him I'm not who he thinks I am. Instead, I enter a stately library in a makeshift dress and with a forged invitation, at a ball where neither I nor my best friend belong.

I pull in a breath as my best friend is left to talk to a sourly royal advisor—and suddenly he's there in the room with me. In my world.

Charles.

The letters on the page lose their grip on me and plunge me back into reality as the weight of his scrutiny hits. Out of the corner of my eye, I watch his stormy gray ones on me.

His features soften as his attention stays on me, and my heart hitches.

I want him to look at me like that longer. I want more of the gentleness I felt in his touch last night.

I don't understand why I want it, or him. I know I don't need more than a friendship with him, and I don't want more.

Except, when I lift my head, I know more than friendship paints my features.

I look up into his face, just as his eyes turn hard and his jaw tightens.

"Good morning."

The ice filling my stomach at his changed mood doesn't echo in my voice. I already feel the first tingles of rejection, and I haven't asked a thing of him.

His lips tilt in a smile, but worry stays in the set of his shoulders, and unease is banked deep in his eyes.

Does he read my features as easily as I read his? Did he see the smattering of hope across my nose and realize that I might want more?

"Your face."

I brush my fingers across my cheek, skin warming with embarrassment.

"My face? What's wrong with it?"

Please don't let there be any remnants of my breakfast. I'm going to be mortified if I've been walking around all morning with crumbs of bread stuck to my face.

"It changes as you read. Just like when you listen to my stories."

A triumphant grin splits my face, because I know what he's talking about now.

"I told you. Reading a book is just like listening to a story."

"Aye, you did tell me. But I didn't believe you."

I pout my lips and make a face of mock consternation.

But he doesn't chuckle like I expect, instead his attention catches on my pout. His eyes trace my lips and tingles spread across my skin as if the look he gives me is a touch.

The sparks I haven't wanted to feel fan into flame. But it's not a fire I can nourish.

Love is not for you.

I press my lips into a line and force my attention back to my book.

I'm not reading nearly enough if I already want more from him. If I want more from him at all.

I've sworn to never again fall in love with someone. It just isn't worth it. Can't be worth it.

It's why I keep my head, and heart, buried in my favorite stories.

And somehow the stories are losing their grip. Or are they?

The nights I've spent in fictional company for so long are now days spent listening to seafaring tales. From a man who has either lived them all or is certifiably insane.

The same man standing in front of me now with a frown etched on his face that I want so badly to erase.

I shouldn't want to erase it, and I absolutely shouldn't try.

But can I?

I'm barely an acquaintance of his, at the most a new friend. Nothing so serious as my heart wants.

Would he share with me if I were to ask what bothers him?

Has he ever shared his thoughts with anyone that way?

Was he ever married?

"Did you ever have a wife?"

I blurt the question out before my brain is fully aware of what we're doing.

Oh God, did I just say that out loud?

Heat burns in my cheeks as I avert my gaze from his. How could I have let that question slip out?

"I'm so sorry, I didn't mean to... I mean, I shouldn't have—"

"I have never had a wife. I have no loyalty to give a woman."

His clipped words take me by surprise, and despite my mortification, I look at him. The hard set of his jaw is back, but in his eyes I see...pain?

He doesn't seem like a disloyal man. It's only been two weeks since I first laid eyes on him, but it's not at all my impression of him.

The events of the night before last crowd into my mind. The tender way he held me as I cried all over him after he rescued me. His choice to follow me to make sure I made it home safely.

I speak the words before I've finished the thought.

"I don't think I've ever had a friend as loyal as you."

He looks at me, and his eyes narrow. But I can't read him, and his lips don't move, neither to dispute my words nor elaborate on his.

And this is why I can't allow any more sparks to be fanned into flames. It's why I can't ever let the hope I felt earlier form into a question.

Because the mere realization that this friendship growing between us must end terrifies me.

Like all fairytales, this one will fade too. And I'll be pulled back to reality as the covers close around another perfect story.

Pain etches into my heart, so sharp it draws a gasp from me.

"What's wrong?"

His eyes are soft again as he steps closer, and I want to shield my heart.

His hand reaches out as if to touch me. But he doesn't.

I wave away his concerns, shut my eyes from the ones that sometimes seem to see right through me. To the parts of me that need to stay hidden.

"I'm fine."

The lie fills the room. It stretches, tangles with the sunlight, makes itself at home around us.

I speak to drown it out.

Voicing the first idea that splatters into my distraught brain.

"Would you like to go on a daytrip with me? There's an island not far from here. We can take the speed ferry and walk around on the beach? I think you'd like it."

I think you'll love it.

I hold my breath as he mulls it over, unable to read his eyes.

"I have no coin for the ferry."

I push out a breath of relief. That's an easy problem to fix.

"You won't need any. This is my thank you. For the night before last."

A frown crowds his forehead.

"You already thanked me."

"I'd like to do more."

This is not a lie.

But thanking him isn't exactly what's on my mind.

I want more of his arms around me, more of his lips against my hair. More of him, in all the ways I shouldn't.

Last night is seared in my memories, but not for the reasons it should be.

The unease of being harassed is what I should remember. I should vow never to walk home in the dark again.

But I don't. I'm not.

I only need to close my eyes to feel his arms wrapped around me, the warmth of his chest against my wet cheek. His breath on my hair.

For a girl whose protectors have all left, last night was a moment of fantasies.

One I'll visit for years to come. When he's gone.

Pain moves in my chest again, burrowing deep, hollowing it out.

"Treasure, I would be honored to come with you."

I startle, I've almost forgotten that I asked him to come out to the island with me.

But he wants to, and relief slides through my limbs as excitement flutters in my chest. It feels out of character to want to share as much as possible with him before he's gone, but I do.

"Great! Is now good?"

It's too eager, I know. I'm too impulsive, and I've always been.

But there's no reproach in his eyes. Instead, a grin splits his face, and his eyes sparkle as they meet mine.

"Now is good."

Side by side we move down the stone steps of the library stairs. I answer his questions as we walk down the sidewalk.

I open my car door and, after a moment's hesitation, he takes a seat. He watches me, a little too intently, as I buckle up. And then he does the same.

Sunlight darts across the dashboard and the man who fills my heart fills the car too. His body is larger than anyone I've ever driven in this car. But his presence looms larger still.

"You're quiet."

"Just excited to show you this."

And I am.

I smile at him, and it's almost genuine. It has to be.

Because nothing is wrong. All is as it always is. As it always will be.

Shadows fall across the road as we drive through a stretch of woods with turning leaves.

We are friends now, yes. But soon? Soon it will end. Like every other fairytale in my life, he will move on. The covers need to close, and I'll need to find a different story to occupy my heart.

Captain Charles Seewell will go back to his own world—wherever that is.

And I…

I will be here. Alone.

CHAPTER 12

Because when a man
says I'm going home,
he should be heading
for the sea.
—COLLEEN HOOVER

Tress

Captain Charles Seewell is the embodiment of adventure where he stands on the deck of the speed ferry. Tall and sure-footed, with the open ocean spread out in front of him. Wild wind whips his hair around his face. His strong, tanned hands rests on the metal railing, and his gray eyes sparkle.

It is the way I pictured him from the moment we met.

Even between the shelves of the library, surrounded by domesticated books and wall-to-wall carpet, he'd seemed like he belonged out on the water. At the helm of a ship.

Or at its railing. Like this.

Blue waters stretch out in front of us as far as the eye can see. The color of the ocean mirrors the clear blue of the September sky.

The wind pushes white lace of sea foam atop every wave, presses our bodies from every side. Every breath of air tastes like salt.

But I can't take my eyes off of him.

For the first time since we met, he seems truly at ease. Contentment is the only word to describe the expression on his face. His shoulders are relaxed, the coiled tension I've come to associate with him is nowhere to be seen.

The speed at which we whip through the water must be very different from what he was used to in his old life. If his memories of seafaring in the 1700s are indeed memories and not contrived delusions.

And I'm starting to wonder if they are indeed memories.

He shows no signs of motion sickness, contrary to several other passengers we've encountered on this short boat ride.

It's not his first time on a boat. Regardless of what his true story is, the sea runs in his veins.

In the two weeks I've known the man by my side, he hasn't been given to frequent smiles. But the one he gives me now is radiant. His eyes sparkle, the brackets on either side of his lips deepens. The flash of teeth has me unprepared, and my heart catches.

"I thank you, Miss Hayden."

The words are ordinary, but the way his eyes hold mine feels anything but.

Like I'm all he sees.

The chatter of tourists and squeals of children fade to the background. The glitter of the sunlight on the waves dulls.

All I see is him.

The crinkling corners at his eyes deepen, and he looks at me as if he has the ability to caress my skin from afar.

I close my eyes, but when I open them, he is still there.

His presence feels like the proverbial piece of me I've been missing all my life.

I can't trust my judgment, I know this. I once felt this way about Jonah, and until this moment, I would have sworn the part of me that could love like this broke alongside my heart.

This rugged sea captain, whose very existence was unknown to me a short week ago, steps closer to me.

His hand closes around mine on the railing.

I can't breathe.

For five long years I've clung to my broken heart like a vinyl shower curtain clings to a wet body. But somehow the strong fingers pushing their way between mine makes me lose my hold on it.

I don't know who I am without a broken heart.

I was a brokenhearted girl, a brokenhearted teenager, wholehearted just for those few years with Jonah.

Since the love of my life walked out on me, I've held on to that title. The girl with the broken heart.

I look down at our entwined fingers, his thick, tanned ones dwarf mine.

The biting wind off the ocean melts against my heated face.

I used to think real love existed somewhere out there. That if I could only find it, it would keep me safe. But the man who proved to me I was worthy of love was the same man who kicked me to the curb just a few years later.

How do you recover from something like that?

You don't.

Or at least I didn't think you did.

But as I look into Charles Seewell's weathered face, as his stormy eyes darken and drop to my lips?

His calloused fingers touch my jaw with utter tenderness, slide into my hair, and pull me close to him.

His breath mingles with mine.

Each rapid breath.

I didn't think you could recover from the heartbreak that was mine.

But when his lips touch mine?

As his mouth covers mine and splits the stars behind my eyes into shimmery stardust?

I'm not so sure.

The world tilts with his lips against mine. The borders of time and space burst, shatter, and come back together.

"Treasure."

The word on his lips is both my name and his endearment.

The depth of emotion in his voice curls around the bleeding pieces of my heart I've cradled for so long.

With the cold metal railing against one side, and Charles's warm body against my front, I inhale as if I've held my breath all these years.

The air expands painfully in my chest. My hair whips in the wind. Salt meets my tongue as his mouth moves away from mine.

His lips against my eyelids and his warm breath against my cheek are both aphrodisiac and tenderness.

I reach for his jaw, slide my fingertips alongside the rough stubble of his cheek.

He kisses me again, and my resolve floats away on the waves beneath us. Tugged down into oblivion by the currents.

He breaks the kiss, but his arms stay wrapped around me.

My heart pounds in my chest, echoes of his against my ear.

The sea captain I've tried to keep my distance from has broken through defenses meant to stay for a lifetime.

But losing the battle holds no pain.

His hand rubs circles on my back. His lips touch my temple. This kiss, unlike the other, is so tender. So sweet.

My heart sighs, as if it knows when to surrender.

But I?

I'm terrified he isn't real, and equally terrified he is.

CHAPTER 13

Charles

I shouldn't have kissed her.

I was caught up in the feeling of seaspray against my skin. Drunk on my first glimpse of open water since that cursed book flung me to this place with clouds feathered as if over water, but where I could not lay eyes on it.

The small vessel plunged through the waves in a way that defied logic, but it was the ocean all the same.

The great deep that called me to adventure so many years ago, and whose call has never left me.

And she brought it to me.

Treasure.

The sweet expression on her face as I turned to thank her made it impossible not to touch her. Her warm fingers between mine whetted an insatiable hunger for more of her skin.

I lost myself in the softness of her jaw, her silky hair.

And I kissed her.

She hasn't said anything since we left the vessel, her eyes lingering everywhere but on me. As if the sandy shore of the little island we've made landfall on is the most fascinating place she's ever encountered.

It might be.

But it can't be very different from the opposing shore where, from our conversations, she has lived all her life.

I didn't mean to kiss her, and I regret having done so.

Is regret the feeling that reigns in her too?

I follow her down the harbor where stone steps deliver us onto the sand.

We stand side by side. She watches the ocean while I watch her.

Even with the great deep calling to me, the foam of legends lapping at the sand by her feet, I can't keep my eyes from returning to her.

She is movement even when she is still. She toes the sand with her shoe, and slender fingers trace the seam of her shirt. Her chest rises and falls with her breaths. Her lips move—half pursing, half pressing into a tight line.

I can't read her expression, and I shouldn't want to.

"Do I owe you an apology, Treasure?"

Her bottom lip drops, and she turns so swiftly her feet

tangle with the uneven ground and she almost falls.

Her eyes meet mine, searching.

For what?

She swallows, nostrils flaring, eyes burning with a fire I don't recognize.

"Don't you dare apologize."

Her voice is a hiss if it's a whisper.

"You don't regret the kiss?"

She shakes her head, and the relief that slides through me takes me by surprise. And as quickly as it appears, I push it down.

I might not be able to curb what Treasure Hayden does to my heart, but I can keep my hands to myself. From now on.

"You do."

It's not a question, and I know my face must show my true feelings.

Her eyes shimmer with moisture. She lets out a shuddering breath, and I know she's close to tears. I'm taken aback at what it does to me.

"Why did you kiss me if you didn't want to do it?"

"I wanted to. But I shouldn't have."

An apology is at the tip of my tongue, but she made it clear she didn't want one, and there I can pacify her at least.

The tear that slides down her cheek tugs painfully at something in my chest.

I curse at the sight of it.

Treasure lifts her head abruptly at the sound.

I do apologize for that, whether she likes it or not.

When a sniffle reaches me, I can't take it any longer.

I open my arms to her and, after a moment's hesitation, she comes.

I know I need to tell her the truth. Sooner rather than later.

"I haven't been quite honest with you."

She stiffens in my arms but makes no move to leave.

"You're married."

The startling words are mumbled into my shirt, where her breath warms my skin underneath the fabric.

"What? I've never been married."

"Oh. I thought maybe that's why you regretted... Never mind."

She thinks my regret is because I've been unfaithful?

I laugh at that.

"I was never the faithless one."

If I had been, perhaps Sarah Monroe had been right to do as she did. But I never strayed from the promises I made her. Not before I came home to find her buried beneath her father's turf.

"No. I need to tell you the reason I asked you to help me read."

I look over Treasure's head to the ocean behind her. It lies there still and ominous even as the sun glitters off the blue surface.

I don't want to tell her this part of my quest. She's beautiful, but that doesn't make her trustworthy.

Sarah Monroe was beautiful. Samson's Delilah was beautiful. And they were both rotten to the core.

I draw deeply of the air, pungent with the smell of salt and rotting seaweed.

"Treasure, I need to return to my ship. If I can find the book that brought me here, if I can read it, perhaps I can find out how to make it bring me back. That is why I need to learn to read."

She shifts in my embrace until she can look up at me.

"Why didn't you tell me?"

"The story of how I made it to your library could have labelled me as in league with the devil where I come from."

"But you did tell me how you came here."

"Did you believe it to be anything but a drunkard's delusions?"

The color in her cheeks is answer enough.

"So you want me to teach you to read well enough to understand a book that's several hundred years old?"

"Yes."

She bites her lip, and it's a struggle to hold my ground, to stay with our conversation, when all I want is to dip my head again and fit my mouth to hers.

I shouldn't entertain the thought of kissing her again. But I've already got her in my arms. How much closer can I toe the line?

Would she let me kiss her again?

"I can't do that."

I frown. She's all but dared me not to apologize for the kiss, but she wants no repeat of it?

Her eyes widen at my frown.

"There's no way I can teach you to read that well, and I'm not even sure if the adult reading program would get you to that level anytime soon."

"Would you be able to read it?"

"Yes."

"And if I were to find it, would you help me, Mistress Hayden?"

"One hundred percent."

"What?"

She ducks her head into my chest, but she can't hide her blush.

"Oh. I mean, yes I will."

When she looks back up her face is still pink.

I want to keep looking at her, be the answer to the question in those shining eyes. Instead, unease slithers through me at the hope on her features. It's not a hope I can fulfill.

"Describe the book to me again."

I clear my throat.

"It is bound in leather, with golden letters across the cover."

I let her go to size up the book with my hands.

She's right. With the scant progress I've made in her lessons it will take me months before I'll be able to decipher any instructions in the book I seek. Longer still to comb the shelves over three stories in her library to find it.

I'm baffled now at the hope I'd entertained when I was first torn from my ship. That I could solve the riddle of literacy and find my own way home.

She has agreed to help me, but the familiarity sprouting between us makes me uneasy. And the longing to spend more time with her is a warning. One as pressing as stormy clouds on the horizon of a blue ocean.

Danger accompanies sharing my secret with her, even more than when I kissed her.

That was a lapse in judgement. This is not.

"I'll help you."

The burning desire to pull her close again at those three words is certain demise.

Yet I yield.

I pull her close, and I know the maelstrom that is this woman will be my death.

Because as my arms wrap around her again, I never want to let go.

CHAPTER 14

Tress

There are so many books in the world, so many of them in this library. It's never been a problem for me before.

But then I've never had to search out one specific one without the help of the digital catalogue.

And to find the magic book that moved Charles three-hundred-some years forward in time, I'm going to have to look at every shelf.

If the book is even here.

Is there even a book? What if this wild goose chase leads only to an untreated head injury?

I don't want to believe that.

But the odds that a magical book brought the man I've spent my day off with here, from the stormy waters of the 1700's Atlantic Ocean to the library in my little New England town, are so low.

I don't believe in magic.

I don't even believe in love—certifiable magic if ever there was any.

But here I am, wanting to find the proof that the man that saved me from a predator two nights ago hasn't lost his grip on reality.

But he might have.

It might even be contagious looking at the speed I'm scanning the spines of the books with.

We've both worked our way across several feet of shelves.

I round yet another endcap.

And there he is.

Something stirs in my chest at the sight of him. His strong profile tilted towards the feet of books in front of him. The way his brows pull together as he moves down the aisle away from me.

"Any luck?"

My voice rings out in the stillness, and he sends a side-long glance my way.

"Nay."

The gruffness of his voice pulls on the corners of my lips until I smile.

"Are you laughing at me?"

His rumbling voice shoots tingles of awareness down my spine.

"Wouldn't dream of it."

I know my eyes sparkle at him, know the smile on my face is wider than warranted.

But then his chuckle warms the air around us until the books fade and I see only him. Want only him.

Keep wanting him until I replay every sensation of his mouth on mine, his fingers in my hair.

The central heat kicks on, it ticks and rumbles behind the walls, and reality pulls me back.

Finding this book is to let him go.

It's what I have to do.

Even if he wasn't from a different time, if he didn't have a crew depending on him there, I know he wouldn't stay.

Because I'm not the kind of girl worth staying for.

I've never been.

I watch his back retreat and pretend it does nothing to me.

I draw in a deep breath, pushing away the sore spot in my chest, and start again at the top of the overstock shelf lining the back wall of the basement room.

Books of every size and shape, on hundreds of topics. But not yet a single one leather-bound.

Not a one with magic sparking the air around it.

The only sparks in this place are the ones trickling over my skin every time Charles's voice fills the room.

I drop to my knees to slide my fingers along the titles on the bottom shelf.

Again there's no book matching Charles's description.

"Did you ever see the book after you came here?"

I call the words out in the silence, but his answer comes from close by, behind the books I'm perusing.

"No."

I didn't see a book when he appeared either. Only the one I dropped. The copy of *Jane Eyre* that is now wherever it is that books go when they die.

I get back to my feet and pick a new shelf and try to keep my spirits up.

It's dark when we part ways outside the library, still without having found the book.

I step across the porch floor and pull out my keys.

The lock clicks as I open my front door, and the wood groans as I shut it closed behind me.

And suddenly, this morning on the ferry rushes back into my consciousness.

I've spent my entire day off with him, but those two minutes reign supreme in my brain.

I can't believe he kissed me.

I can't believe I let him.

My breath is a gasp as I press my trembling fingers to my lips.

I might have been stoic when we stood on the island beach, drawn a semblance of peace from the water stretching far out before my eyes.

But now? In my own front room away from prying eyes? Away from him?

Here my legs tremble as I drop my bag on the couch, and kick my sneakers off until I'm standing in my socks.

Because it wasn't just a kiss. Not the way his lips moved past my defenses and anchored in my heart.

I can feel him still.

His firm, tender grip on my soul.

Maybe he didn't mean to leave them. The pieces of him dug so deeply into my flesh.

But I know how much it hurts to rip those anchors out, the bleeding mess it leaves behind.

How long it takes to mend. How much it never does.

I lean back against my closed front door. Drop my head back and close my eyes.

And his face is right there, his eyes calling me forth, the tilt of his lips holding me in place.

This is the thing I promised myself I wouldn't do. That I would never do again.

True love is a fairytale.

Love is not for you.

I know this. If I didn't know it before Jonah, surely I've learned it since?

After Lucas I must have.

And still I put myself in this situation. Still my anchored heart crashes violently against my ribs and fear claws at my heart.

I can't do this.

I'm not strong enough to have a man like Charles Seewell kiss me, look at me with tenderness in his eyes, or call me his treasure.

Or sink his claws into my heart.

My head feels light, and my tongue is too large for my mouth.

Panic crashes into my chest, snarls around my airways, squeezes my breastbone until I'm certain it will crack.

I sink to the floor, my back to the door, as my eyes seek out the objects visible from my spot on the floor. I touch my fingers to the cool laminate floor. Listen to the ticking of a clock somewhere. Smell the bourbon vanilla candle on the mantle. Taste the gum I chewed on the way home.

I gasp for air.

I find it and bury my head in my hands.

How pathetic is this?

The most handsome man I've ever known kisses me and I have a full-blown panic attack.

I urge my breath to calm.

Anxiety, you are welcome here.

I repeat the phrase Chris taught me. I may not have had money to spend on my own therapist, but I've benefited hugely from hers.

Normally the words help.

If the pain doesn't leave my chest, it settles.

But this time there's no settling peace, no slowing breath. My blood still thunders through my everything.

And I know why.

This isn't just anxiety. It's a premonition.

I can't handle him leaving, and yet I know he will.

"I'll help you."

My own promise haunts me. I will help him. If it kills me.

And when he leaves? It just might.

CHAPTER 15

Tress

The ancient book on the shelf in front of me matches the description Charles has given me to a tee. The worn, but clearly gilded, letters splayed across the leather cover call to me.

We've spent another three days searching for the book he believes pulled him out of his ship's cabin and into my library almost three weeks ago.

I didn't really expect to find it, at least not randomly laid out on a shelf like this.

I glance again at the book. It has no library markings.

This must be it.

The book I've found must be the very one Charles has been talking about.

A tremble goes through my hand as I touch my fingertips to the soft leather.

I pull them away immediately, but the damage is done.

The groaning of a ship's hull fills the air, followed by the sound of ocean waves and faint men's voices.

It's eerily like the sounds that filled the room in the instant before Charles appeared.

My head spins, and I stand frozen to the spot.

He doesn't have a head injury.

It really was a book that pulled him out of his own world, tossing him cruelly into mine.

I can no longer entertain my ideas about his delusions. Or mine.

I saw him standing there submerged in sea water that had no plausible reason to be in the basement of a library. But until now, I didn't fully believe he had really been nabbed from his captain's cabin and deposited here.

With all the proof one could expect, I still hadn't really believed him until now.

His footsteps sound around the corner, and I brace for the pain I know will come.

The book I've found means it's time to say goodbye.

The thought of his leaving towers over me. There is no future for him here, but the mournful sound that rises up in my chest cries with the lone voice of the sea.

"Treasure!"

Charles shouts my name, and I notice the trickle of water from the book.

I twist my head away from the steady stream to look at him.

There's fear in his eyes.

In another moment, his strong arms close around my middle and he curses close to my ear.

I can't move, but not because of his arms around me.

He can't move me either.

Water gushes around us. The chill reaches to my bones. And the salt stings my eyes.

"Charles!"

I gasp his name, because I can't feel him anymore.

I can't even feel the floor of the library under my feet.

A mouthful of saltwater slides down my throat, and my stomach threatens to heave.

I flail in the icy water.

So much water. Where is the surface? Where is Charles?

Panic claws at the last dregs of my consciousness.

Something slips around my ankle. A tentacle? Rope?

I can't tell.

I can only tell that it's stronger than me and pulling me down, down into the dark depths of water below me.

The freezing blackness closes around me.

I know this will be my last thought.

I'm throwing up. Bile and saltwater burns my throat. I heave again, and strong fingers brush away the hair that is plastered to my face.

I'm on the floor of the library, but I must still be out of it, because it seems to be moving. Creaking.

I try to sit up, but the hands by my face move to hold me back.

"Easy, Treasure."

Charles.

"Oh my God what happened?"

He doesn't answer.

I'm suddenly aware that we're not alone. Also that I'm freezing.

My clothes are slicked to my skin, and my teeth are chattering. I'm laid on the floor in a puddle of water.

I'm going to die from embarrassment when my coworkers discover me.

Or have they already?

Disembodied voices float to me on the breeze.

Breeze?

I scrunch my forehead as I try to make sense of the cool air on my face.

Footsteps near me across the plank floor. The world tilts sideways once more, and my body makes another attempt to expel the contents of my stomach.

"Captain?"

Captain? No one at the library knows of Charles's identity but me, and not even I call him captain.

Vise-like pain hammers my head as I try to grasp the full picture of what's happening.

"I'll take her below."

Below where?

I roll to my back, trying not to wince at the thought that I might be rolling in puke. Shooting pain flashes through my temples as I open my eyes to stare up into the...very blue skies showing through the rigging.

And I scream.

I'm hoisted into the air as if I weigh nothing and pressed against a hard, wet chest. The rumble of Charles's voice as he spouts off orders calms me a fraction.

"I don't understand what's happening? Please tell me this isn't happening."

I blubber the words through the tears that overflow my eyes and move in fiery paths down my cold cheeks.

Charles carries me across the deck and ducks down into the dark underbelly of what can't possibly be a ship. He holds me steady down the steps, and we're plunged into darkness.

No, not complete darkness.

There's some light from the doorway to the deck.

A stale, musty smell, like old food and rotten seawater, assaults my nose. And I want to close my eyes and ears so I can't see the grimy beams above us or hear the creaking of the ship around us.

My skin feels wrong. My throat tightens. My breath comes faster than my lungs will expand.

"Treasure, you're going to make yerself faint."

"Please tell me what's happening."

I whimper the words and close my eyes so tightly my face hurts.

I hope against hope that when I open them, my cheek will rest against the blue polyester carpet in the library basement.

"We went back."

Back where?

Another doorway and he deposits me on a bed in what is decidedly a ship's cabin.

We have gone back.

To his world.

To the place where Captain Charles Seewell is not a homeless man hanging out at the library. To a place where I was never meant to be.

Terror grips me, and I can't push it away. Tears wet my cheeks again.

Charles bends to dig through a chest a few feet away. He stands and hands me what I assume is clothing.

"You'll need to get out of your wet clothes. Can you undress yourself?"

I shiver, and I think the answer is no.

I nod.

"I'll leave you to it. Don't take too long."

"Why?"

The word is raspy, and I no longer recognize my voice.

"So you won't catch sickness, and so I don't walk back in while you're indecent."

Should I be embarrassed at that thought?

My brain is too foggy to care. I move my head in a nod instead.

He leaves the cabin, without another glance backward.

I sit in a daze for another minute.

What if he makes good on his threat?

I pull my drenched clothing off.

My fingers are almost numb, and my chattering teeth hurt my head.

This has to be a dream. A hallucination.

What did I eat or drink in the last day? Did someone spike my tea over lunch?

I slip into the large, stiff garments he's provided me with, then tie the belt rather than buckling it.

I'm not wearing women's clothing. Both the shirt and pants seem made for a man much taller and broader than me. The man whose world I'm suddenly inhabiting.

I've spent years terrified of falling in love and equally terrified of dying from loneliness. But the terror I feel now is different.

I look around the ship's cabin that should not be here.

A lamp dangles from the ceiling, and several chests are bolted to the floor against the opposite wall from the bed. The large, ornate desk in the middle of the room looks like it belongs on a plantation, not on a lowly pirate ship. But pirates are rich, aren't they? From plundering.

I'm on a ship full of criminals.

Fear clogs my throat, and terror lodges painfully in my chest.

My mouth feels as if it's full of cotton, and my lungs don't expand quite like I'd like them to.

I pull in a breath that hurts my shoulders. Pressure mounts on my breastbone, and I rub it hard.

Breathe, Tress.

I pull in another forceful breath, and another. The pain in my chest makes me whimper and my head feels light. Too light.

I can't pass out.

Don't pass out.

Slowly the pressure in my chest eases. But it doesn't go away.

I'm stuck on a ship, somewhere in the past. I'm in a situation that shouldn't exist, and for the first time in my life, I don't know if I'll make it out alive at all.

CHAPTER 16

Charles

I close the door to my cabin, and my mind spins. Treasure Hayden is on my ship. My feet are once again on the lower deck of the Lady Monroe—the vessel I thought I'd never see again.

I tear off my soaked clothes.

Enough time had passed since I last saw my ship, I'd thought I'd need to find employment in her world while searching for the book.

Surely there'd be work for a skilled sailor in the harbors of her town?

But here, Will says, only hours have passed since he last saw me. Enough for him to have found my cabin empty, but not enough to count me lost when none had seen me go overboard.

I wring the icy water out of my garments and hang them over an empty barrel, before I pull on the dry clothes I grabbed from my chest.

Against my wildest hopes, Treasure found the magical book.

I close my eyes and rest my head against the wall. The sounds that assaulted me as I rounded the corner in her library are the same ones around me now—the creaking of masts and the loud flapping of canvas in the wind.

The sight of her, standing in the middle of a maelstrom of seawater pierced me with terror like I'd never felt.

The book releasing the flood was the same I remembered from my cabin, but there had not been this much water last time. Even a strong swimmer could easily succumb to a current as strong as the one I'd watched her caught in.

I open my eyes to escape the terror of moments ago, pick up my sodden clothes, and toss them at the nearest crewman passing me on his way to fulfil my orders.

The same woman I carried easily in my arms moments ago had been as immovable as a rooted tree in the middle of the water pouring forth from the book. I'd locked my arms around her and hauled with my full strength, and she hadn't moved.

And then she'd been gone. Darkness had closed around us and saltwater had burned my eyes. Shouting her name had yielded nothing but a burning throat and a belly full of seawater.

I'd surfaced to a familiar railing lined with faces, bellowed my first mate's name, and I'd ducked back into the churning waters.

I'd searched frantically in the dark water, and when her stockinged foot had appeared as if by magic, I'd closed my hand around her ankle.

Her wild kicking had ceased only with the loss of her consciousness, and I'd pulled her to the surface as Will's body hit the water. In the next moment he'd been by my side with the rope he'd dived in with.

She'd been as limp as a soaked rag when my men had hauled her over the railing. Their faces had been pale as they watched their captain reappear from the ocean after disappearing for who knows how long.

I knock on the door to my own cabin. The cabin boy awaiting my orders shoots me a strange look, but my scowl makes his eyes lower fast.

If I hadn't known before that leaving her behind was the only option, I know now. The memory of my crewmen's leering grins as their roving eyes passed over Treasure's barely clothed form is enough to make anger burn in my chest. They may have questioned how she'd come to be in the middle ocean, but not enough to avert their eyes.

I open the door, relieved to see her body hidden by the clothes I handed her before I left.

Perhaps in her world her outfit would be considered modest, but not here. And not drenched in seawater.

I close the door behind me, cross the room, and kneel at her feet.

Her pale skin and glassy eyes worry me. And the small, shivering hand I cradle in mine is so cold.

"Treasure."

Her bluish lips press into a firm line, and her eyes meet mine.

"I don't know what to do."

Neither do I, but from the despair in her voice, it isn't what she needs to hear.

"Are you in pain?"

She shakes her head, but more tears well in her eyes and follow the tracks of former ones down her cheeks.

"How will I get back?"

"I don't know."

I raise my hand to her cheek, and she rests her face against my palm.

"You're so cold."

I sit on my bed next to her and pull her up into my lap. If she finds the position too intimate she doesn't say so.

I wrap my hands around her bare feet. Her skin is like ice. I squeeze her foot, careful not to rub the skin, and she relaxes against me. The shivers wracking her body ease a little.

She can't be here, but she is.

From the moment she tempted my heart to beat again, I had known I could never subject Treasure to the life I led before meeting her. If I could even find my own way back, I'd have to leave her.

And now she's in the middle of the dangerous life I'd hoped to shield her from.

Women don't belong at sea, and I have no other home. Perhaps a few years ago, when pirates had the support of the colonies, I could have gone back on land. Like I had planned to with Sarah.

But marauders are hanged in droves these days.

Perhaps I'm not infamous, but a gallows awaits me if I step foot in the wrong port. And a lone woman, worse the remains of a pirate, would suffer. I have no relatives, no one who might keep her safe when I can't.

148

I wrap my arms around her and she rests her cheek against my chest.

Dry clothes and the heat of my body will solve the most direct threat she's facing—illness from being submerged in the icy waters of the ocean. It will do nothing at all to save her from every other threat she's now facing.

I'd divulged some of my life at sea to her over the last weeks, and she'd shown me the drawings of pirates in her books for children. Caricatures that hold no candle to the horrors of pirate life in these waters.

She moves on my lap, tilting her face until she looks up at me. Her soft skin and wide eyes call to me.

It makes me wonder like I did so many times in her world...

Is she that temptress meant to tempt me to stay with Hades like I'd first thought?

But with her here, now, she can't be.

I allow myself to brush a kiss against her temple.

By the railing of the ferry days ago, I couldn't have resisted the kiss I'd stolen if Poseidon himself had stood over her to deny me. But here I can, because I know I should have never brought her to this place.

I should have resisted that time too. And I'd thought I'd be able to, until she looked at me as if I was her home and she was more than willing to be mine.

She was always meant to stay in the safety of her own world. It might hold occasional dangers, but nothing like what she'll face here.

I need to get her back to her own world.

CHAPTER 17

Charles

The rhythmic movements of the ship tugs me from my sleep. Voices from the crew's quarters drift through the space.

I push myself up from my position on the plank floor outside the door to my cabin. My back and legs protest as I stand up. I groan and rub my aching neck.

I don't miss the bed I had in Treasure's world, but I do miss knowing she's sleeping soundly in hers.

I don't regret letting Treasure take my bed in the cabin, but from the sobs I heard last night, I doubt she slept much.

She needs to go back.

I want her here, more than I should. I want to be able to wrap her in my arms again like I did last night. But without her crying, and for longer. I want to stay in that cabin with her. Spend my nights listening to her soft breathing, and my days with her right here by my side.

But none of that is to be.

The life I lead can't be shared with a woman. And even if it could, she belongs in a world wildly different from mine.

And I can't take that from her.

I need to knock on that cabin door and find out how to send her back to her own world.

I raise my hand to knock, and the metal key around my neck burns against my chest.

I hesitate a moment too long, and footsteps sound down the ladder.

I turn towards the sound just as a lanky crewman's long legs eat up the short distance and stop in front of me.

"First Mate wants the Captain to know we're close to port."

I need to talk to Will.

Maybe I can hold off that long before talking to Treasure. But even behind a locked door that I alone have the key to, I don't trust her safety on this ship.

I trust several of my men, and Will most of all, but there are exceptions. After the strange things that have happened to us in these waters, I'll take no chances with Treasure.

Can I ask the man in front of me to guard her door?

But the crewman awaiting my message is one we picked up in a port not too long ago. Not one I'd trust with the precious cargo in my cabin.

His message finally penetrates the fog in my brain.

"Port, you say?"

I left the helm to Will after the last dogwatch when we'd been in the middle of the ocean. Too far from dry land to have reached the coast already.

"Yes, Captain, we are closing in on Newport."

Unease flickers in his eyes, and I know it's a mirror of mine. Newport is bad news, but for more reasons than this man knows.

The woman in my cabin depends on me, but if we are truly in Newport, I will fail her.

I can't get Treasure back to her own world if we are no longer anywhere close to the Triangle of Spirits.

"Tell your first mate I'll be up."

The crewman nods and leaves.

And I wish I could join him.

Anything but see her blue eyes tear up when I tell her I will not send her back to her home.

I can't risk the cursed waters where I was sucked into her world again, if we have escaped them. Not even to bring her back.

Worse things than traveling through time lurk in the depths of that place, and I can't risk all of our lives, twenty-eight souls to traverse them again.

Only one ship I know of has sailed through the Triangle and been seen again, with neither crewmen nor sanity lost—mine.

If we have been seen again.

Is this port not Newport, but a fairy port?

I need to talk to my first mate, but I need to see her more.

I knock on my cabin door.

"Yes?"

Just her voice is enough to calm the thoughts racing through my head.

"It's me. I'm coming in."

I wait, but when she doesn't speak, I unlock the door and step inside.

Treasure sits on the bed. My clothes drown out any sign of her true figure. Relief drops my shoulders.

But Treasure does not look relieved. Her eyes are red and her hair messy.

My chest tightens at the thought that I'll bring her even more pain.

"Did you sleep?"

She shrugs. "Not much."

The lost expression on her face makes me want to fold her back into my arms and tell her that all will be well. But it's far from the truth, and so I don't.

I glance at my desk. The cursed book sits there just like it did moments before I was sucked out of my time.

Treasure's eyes follow mine.

"I already tried it. It's just a book."

"What do you mean you tried it?"

Terror clenches in my chest, and my voice comes out sharper than it should.

Has she really attempted to go back without letting me know?

"I touched it, and nothing happened."

I bite back the order I want to bark at her. She's not my crewman, and scaring her into obedience will do neither of us any good.

I take a step back.

"I need to talk to Will, and I need you to stay here until I know what is going on."

She nods.

My arms ache for her, and worried I'll sweep her into my embrace again, I leave the cabin.

I lock the door behind me, and wait for my cabin boy to return to guard it before I take the steps up into the sunlight two at a time. My strides eat up the planks of the deck until I stand at the railing. But the smooth wood under my hands brings me none of the comfort I normally feel when overlooking the ocean from the railing of my ship.

The crewman didn't lie.

Barely visible, spread out in front of me is a port I recognize. The same one I dreamed of during the years I stayed away, plundering merchant's ships and saving up for a farm.

Newport was Sarah Monroe's port.

But Sarah's soul is long departed from this earth, and it's been a mere two years since twenty-three pirates were tried and hanged in this very port.

Newport is not a place I can safely step foot. Neither is it a place where I can bring the woman staying put in my cabin. I can't keep her safe here.

And if I can't keep her safe, who will?

"Will!"

I bark his name even before I reach him.

"How are we closing in on Newport this morning when we were on the open ocean last night?"

He grins and shakes his head.

"I don't know, Captain, but I'm glad to be out of the cursed waters. Even if it's here."

He turns and spits behind his shoulder.

Newport is not my first choice either.

"We can't pass, Captain. The mainsail is torn, and we're low on supplies."

"I know."

Will nods, as if he's already resigned to anchoring up in this cursed port. Then mischief sparks in his eyes.

"Who's the girl, Captain? I heard you slept on the floor outside your cabin."

"She wasn't meant to come here."

"No?"

"No."

Will is my first mate and best friend, but I can't share with him where I've been. If the wrong person was to overhear, I would risk a mutiny. Captains have lost their ships for less, and my story would make anyone judge my mind as overcome with madness.

"So, she's a…friend?"

"Yes."

"That's why you looked ready to murder me when I dared look her way yesterday?"

"Her clothes were soaked through."

"I noticed." Will smirks.

My elbow connects with his gut, and he lets out a grunt.

"You'll speak about her with respect, understood?"

Will shakes his head, his smile still in his eyes if not on his lips.

"Yes, Captain."

"We'll drop anchor tonight."

In a port where if we draw too much attention to ourselves we'll be doomed. But I have no other choice.

We are out of supplies and going ashore can't be helped. And I have more than my ship to think about.

I need to protect the woman waiting in my cabin. Until I have a plan for how to do that, I'll need to keep her close.

She's going to have to come ashore.

CHAPTER 18

Tress

"They hang pirates in this port."

I try to concentrate on the rest of Charles's words, but the terror that gripped me at his first sentence won't let go. It crashes around in my chest like a real, living thing.

Salty wind tosses my hair and rapid waves toss my stomach.

Newport, Rhode Island is not known for executions in my time. Not of pirates or anyone else.

But the year I saw scrawled in the captain's log I found in his desk is centuries removed from the year I wrote in my journal last night.

1725.

I want to be sick.

Charles is still talking by the railing next to me, but it's as if I no longer understand him.

I close my eyes wanting to shut out the bustling harbor we're closing in on. But we're nowhere near it yet.

I can't yet hear voices, shouts, or laughter. I can't smell the stench of sweating bodies, the rotting wood and water I'm sure will soon assault my senses, but it makes no difference.

In my mind it's already upon us.

I grip the railing with a hand that has gone weak and push down the nausea.

Why are we stopping in this port when it's so dangerous?

How can he be so flippant with his life? With mine?

There is no way for me to get back without Charles's help. I always knew he would one day leave me, but I didn't know it could be as gruesome as this.

If he is caught, if he is…

I can't even think it.

A scene from a pirate movie I once watched trickles through my mind. Paid actors whose filthy half-dressed bodies dangle by their necks from ropes swaying in the Caribbean breeze.

I close my eyes, desperate to avoid where my imagination will take me next.

I shudder as the faces in my memories change, and all I see is him.

Charles's bronzed skin and long hair. The smile lines at the corners of his eyes, his lips tugged in a grin.

But not like that.

In the vision torturing the insides of my eyelids it's no longer the face of the man I've been trying so hard not to want. His beautiful face is empty.

I open my eyes, to look at anything else. I want to throw up.

Even if he never wants me back, I need him desperately in this world.

He's the only reason I'm safe, even here aboard his ship.

"Promise me you won't open this door for anyone but me."

I knew the kind of men he must be employing on his ship. I never expected them to be upstanding citizens, but still they're worse than I imagined.

The way he's locked the cabin door behind him every time he's left, making me promise to let in only him, speaks volumes about how much he trusts his crew. And how much danger I'm in when I'm not with him.

I'm not safe here. Not in this world or on his ship. Maybe he will protect me when we are together, but if he's not here? If he can't?

I'll be alone, and in danger. Well over 260 years before I was born.

My favorite books haven't even been written.

Jane Austen won't be born for another century, and when she is, it will be an ocean away.

This America is nothing like the one I've known all my life. I shudder with what I know of life in colonial times.

A whimper passes my lips.

"Treasure?"

Charles's voice barely penetrates my thoughts.

Is there really any way for me to survive here? A single woman with no connections?

It's difficult enough three centuries from now, but in this one?

Perhaps I will be married off sooner rather than later, but it won't be the marriage I've always wanted.

Not the fantasy I've immersed myself in in historical novels.

It will be a marriage of necessity, not of love.

Bile rises in my throat, and I clap a hand to my mouth.

"Treasure, are you unwell? Did you hear what I said?"

I shake my head and it makes my throat burn with

whatever is left of the stale biscuit I had for breakfast.

I know Charles had nothing, and it will be a poor thanks indeed if I throw up his ration now.

"Can't we wait for another port?"

I meet his eyes. The steely gray is soft with concern as he swallows and measures his next words.

"We're out of supplies. We have no choice but to put down the anchor."

I lower my hand again.

"And you're not going to take into consideration that you might get yourself hanged?"

"I'd have to be caught before I would be hanged. I can't sail this ship without proper supplies. We have repairs that need to be made."

He points to the barely mended tear in the sail above us.

"My crew needs to eat and drink."

I close my eyes, and I don't mean for him to hear my whisper.

"I'm so afraid."

But he does hear, and his arms close around me like bands of steel. False promises of endless warmth and protection. He pulls me to his strong chest, and I want to stay right here forever.

If only he wanted to.

I press my cheek against his shirt. Warm from his body heat it still smells musty, as if it's been stored in a damp place for a long time.

Like in a chest aboard an eighteenth century pirate ship.

Cold reality slithers down my spine. Charles's arms are still tight around me, but they don't keep the terror from sneaking in.

If this is a nightmare I'd like to wake up now.

Charles's voice rumbles through his chest against my ear.

"You can trust me. I will keep you safe."

"But will you keep yourself safe?"

I breathe the words, but the way he stiffens, he must have heard them.

He doesn't answer, only tightens his grip around me.

Because he can't promise me either. If he can't keep himself safe there's no one to do the same for me, and we both know it.

In the three decades I've lived, I have been left behind more often than not by the people who were supposed to stay. The ones who promised to keep me safe.

My parents.

Eon.

Jonah.

Lucas.

Charles is just one more.

One more can't matter.

But the aching chasm that opens in my chest at the thought of losing him? The way I feel as if fear has me suspended in midair even as his arms hold me? Both say one more will be the last straw.

That this time the ache of abandonment will be fatal.

CHAPTER 19

Tress

By nightfall, we drop the anchor.

An argument breaks out onboard about something I don't understand. And honestly, I don't want to know.

There's yelling and pushing, and just the murderous looks on some of the pirates' faces along with the mumbled, and not so mumbled, curses make me happy I'm not in charge of this crew of wild men.

But Charles is.

Unease trickles through me at the thought.

How high is the risk of mutiny really on a ship like this one? With men who look like they are one misstep away from having their throats slit in their sleep by their adversary?

Charles' arm wraps around my shoulders as he leads me below deck, together with Will, who goes unaided.

The cabin door closes behind the three of us, and Charles turns to me.

I don't like the look on his face, and I like his next words even less.

"I'm taking you and Will ashore. If something happens to me, you will stay with Will, do you understand?"

He gestures to the tall towheaded man I know to be his first mate.

I turn my frown back on Charles.

"Can't you have someone else walk ashore? I don't understand why *you* have to go when—"

"Mistress Hayden, do you understand?"

I hope the formality is for Will's sake, but it still feels strange to have him address me like that.

"I understand."

Relief shines in his eyes, and I feel it in the tender touch of his hand as he slides it along my jaw—the formality in front of his crewmember all but forgotten.

"I'd leave you behind if I thought it would be safer. But when you're with me, I can..."

He looks uncomfortable, his glance bouncing off of Will as if he wishes his first mate wasn't here for this part of the conversation.

"I can come up with a story."

Will grins, and I can imagine what kind of story might get me released if his captain is caught.

"As long as you're on my ship there's no denying you're with me. And if I don't come back..."

His eyes shift to Will, and another look passes between them. This one without a trace of humor.

"I met Will Hayle when I was just a lad of fifteen. We boarded our first ship together."

I remember how Charles spoke of Will in my world, and I know this man must be more than just the Lady Monroe's First Mate to him.

Charles doesn't trust his crew with me. I already know this from the crewman posted outside the locked cabin door whenever he's on deck, but their serious faces still make a tingle of fear slide down my spine.

I shudder at the thought of being unsafe even here.

Will and Charles escort me from the cabin under cover of darkness.

I'm still dressed as a man, and I'm thankful for that as Charles moves to climb in front of me down the rope ladder over the side of the ship.

The rowboat looks so miniscule down on the water, rocked back and forth by the forces of invisible waves far, far below us.

"Don't look. It just makes it worse."

Will's voice is half a chuckle in my ear. I jump, and he laughs.

"What are you doing, Will?"

"Nothing, Captain, just helping out."

"...likely that."

Some of the words cut off as he moves further and further down.

"Ready, Miss Hayden?"

I let Will help me over the side of the railing. My fingers tremble as my feet fumble for somewhere to put my weight.

Nothing.

I'm going to die.

There, finally my foot finds the step of the rope ladder. I step down on the next step, then another, and another.

I white-knuckle each wooden rung on my way down.

The dark swallows up the little light from Will's lantern, and I let my hands slide down the rope to the next rung, never completely letting go of the ladder.

My foot hits the unsteady bottom of the boat and Charles's hands are around my waist, steadying me.

I take my first full breath since my feet were on the solid deck.

Charles chuckles.

"Here, move slowly."

His hand guides me to the seat at one end of the boat.

Will is at the bottom of the ladder before I'm seated.

Did he just slide down it?

But I've already seen him climb the rigging on deck as if he's half monkey, so this shouldn't surprise me.

The crewman rowing us ashore begins his task. For a minute the rhythmic splash and slide of the oars is all that fills the air. But not for long.

The Newport harbor isn't quiet even at night, and the sound of the oars is soon drowned out by the nightlife around us.

A cackle of rowdy laughter and off-key, lilting music sounds from a tavern somewhere on shore. An animal whines in the dark.

I hope it's an animal.

As we hit the harbor wall, the rotten smell is enough to turn my stomach.

Squeaks sound from somewhere in the dark, and a shadow skitters along the harbor wall.

I press down a shudder and try not to think about what it might be.

"How are we supposed to get supplies when it's nighttime?"

Somehow that question hasn't occurred to me until now.

"The suppliers I need to see will do so regardless of the hours."

I don't know exactly what Charles means by this, but it would be naive to assume that pirates wouldn't conduct their business with other equally nefarious businesses. Ones whose proprietors wouldn't have anything against operating under the cover of darkness.

On Charles's signal I stand, and Will puts his hands around my waist, as if to lift me out of the boat. A comment from Charles, too quiet for my ears, has his hands dropping swiftly.

Charles places his hands where Will's were a moment ago and lifts me onto the dock. He jumps up after me, and Will follows. Only the crewman who helped row us in stays put.

"Is he not coming?"

Will chuckles at my question.

"No, poor Mose will have to guard the boat. We're not the only ones fond of taking what isn't ours around here."

The stench is even worse on land than it was in the boat. I want to plug my nose, but I don't want to draw attention to myself.

We pass what I'm almost certain is the carcass of a dog, and I shudder.

Charles wraps a warm hand around mine and tugs me close to him.

"What's wrong?"

"The dog."

He glances behind us to the pile of bones and fur. Crawling with things I don't want to know about.

"Our harbors are not as clean as yours."

I snort.

"That's an understatement."

But clean or not, I'm starting to understand that they are the same harbors.

Charles lets go of my hand as he responds to a comment from Will.

I've never been to Newport, Rhode Island despite having lived my whole life less than an hour away. It probably doesn't look like this anymore, but I'd bet a great deal of money that there are buildings here now that are still standing in my time.

I know there are in other local harbors.

Charles's long legs eat up the ground much faster than I can make mine do in my borrowed boots.

"Charles!"

He's already twenty or so feet ahead of me when I call his name.

He turns, and I try to tune out the annoyed protest from Will.

"She's going to slow us down, Captain."

Charles closes the distance between us and grabs my hand again.

His skin is warm and dry against my sweaty palm. I almost slip out of his hand as he hauls me along with him.

We close in on dark buildings where the stench of urine is so strong I'm gagging. How Will and Charles are not, is beyond me.

We pass several wooden houses that look surprisingly modern. Maybe only because there are still so many colonial houses in the area I live. A dark figure huddled between two of them calls out to us.

A man much older than me steps out into our path. The light of a torch illuminates his knee length pants, filthy and torn, and his lack of stockings below them. His once white shirt is dank and yellowed. He leers at me, and I don't need to understand his suggestive words to know it's the reason Charles stiffens and sneers at him.

The man smells so bad that I actually gag, and Will pushes him out of our way. The loud protests from the alleyway follow us as we move away.

I'm clutching Charles's hand so hard my knuckles must be white, but he doesn't seem to notice. To him this is a normal harbor town, with stenches and sounds he's familiar with.

But every unbidden smell that reaches my nostrils makes my stomach roll.

The people we pass on the streets are dressed in colonial fashions, but look significantly less flashy than the pictures I've seen in history books. The women are wearing full skirts, waists stiff with stays, and fichus tucked into them—except for a few, who clearly skipped their modesty shawl for a reason.

To my relief, Charles doesn't pay those women any attention, but I see Will wink at a few of them.

He stops to put his arm around one of them.

"Will, we have work to do."

Charles's words are but a grunt, but the command is clear enough.

Will groans, but let's go of the girl and runs to catch up.

We finally come to a stop in front of what looks to be a tavern, a large wooden building aglow in the lights from inside the open door. The patrons that mill in and out make me very thankful I'm not walking these streets alone.

That's exactly what you'll do if Charles manages to get himself arrested.

Another jolt of fear hits me at the thought, and I squeeze Charles's fingers more tightly.

I don't expect his answering squeeze. Warmth spreads in my chest.

But the smile on my lips is cut short when he drops my hand.

"Stay with Will."

Another clear command. Charles ducks his tall frame under the door beam, pushes past a man stopped on the threshold.

And then he's gone.

CHAPTER 20

Tress

I gape.

"Did he just…leave me alone with you?"

Will snorts.

"He'll be back."

I really hope he will. Because I don't know what I'll do if he doesn't.

An enamored couple bumps me back against Will in their quest to get through the door of the tavern without pausing their make-out session.

Will steadies me, then steps away.

Two girls, way too young to be in a place like this and clearly drunk, stumble across the threshold from the other side, out into the street, laughing hysterically.

They are around the same age as I was when my parents checked out completely.

When Eon had left, and they forgot they still had a daughter.

In 280 some years, if I hadn't already discovered our small-town library, they could have been me.

Sadness seeps through me, and I shiver, even though the night is still humid and warm.

I turn to Will with the question that's been on my lips since Charles disappeared inside the tavern.

"Where did he go?"

Will shrugs.

"Business. The less you know, the better."

He's probably right not to tell me anything. I look around at the motley crowd of people milling about the front doors of this place.

I don't know who could be our enemy out here, and Will probably doesn't either. This time period isn't referred to as "the war on pirates" for nothing.

A loud squeal breaks through the chatter around us.

I turn towards the noise.

One of the young girls is being pressed against the wall of the building by a man much larger than her. She's barely visible behind him, but it's clear that she's struggling.

I can't see what he's doing, but I hear the fear in her voice.

"Stop."

Her voice trembles, and a grunt sounds from the man. "You'll pay for that…"

A shiver runs down my spine at the sinister voice. I look to Will to see if he'll intervene, but he's only staring at them, a blank expression on his face.

The girl lets out a sob, and before I can talk myself out of it, I've closed the distance between us, and I'm next to them.

I barrel my weight into the man. It's enough to put him off balance.

The girl wrenches out of his grasp, and she doesn't need my suggestion to hightail it out of there.

Her friend joins her, and I breathe a sigh of relief.

I realize my mistake just as a fist closes around my upper arm.

"Who do you think you are, whelp? You want to take her place, eh?"

The man's breath stinks, and I catch the glimpse of rotted stubs where his teeth should have been.

I shrink back and tug on my arm to free it, but it might as well have been stuck in hardened concrete.

The sharp reek of alcohol around him probably explains how I was able to move him at all. He's much larger than me. So much larger.

I gulp.

"I..." Am in very deep water.

"Leave him alone, mate. He didn't mean no harm."

Will's voice is jovial, as if this man didn't just threaten to assault me in place of the girl I saved.

"Still cost me the girl. You got another replacement for me?"

I shudder and try to wrench my arm away again.

The man growls and twists my arm.

I can't keep my cry of pain in.

"You little whelp—"

The garbled words are cut off by a resounding crack as Will's fist connects with the man's jaw.

The grip on my arm loosens, and I tear away and jump behind Will.

Another fist grabs me. I whirl around and knee my attacker in the groin.

He lets out a grunt of pain that tells me I made contact exactly as planned, but he doesn't let go of my arm.

And the curse that follows is familiar. Too familiar.

"Did she just..."

Will is gaping at me, and I follow his wide-eyed stare to the man bent over next to me.

Charles.

My stomach shrivels.

"I'm so sorry, I didn't know it was you!"

A snort comes from Will, then a bark of laughter. He's not the only one.

Onlookers are calling out their own insults, and worse, suggestions.

"Come on, man! Give the troublemaker some of his own medicine!"

Several voices, both male and female, chime in to agree.

Of course I'm the troublemaker for trying to save an innocent girl from assault.

Charles groans as he straightens.

"This is you 'not attracting attention', Hayle?"

"She's the one who picked a fight with a man twice her size."

"I'm really sorry. Are you okay?"

Charles doesn't take his eyes off of Will, as if he didn't even hear me.

His voice and face darkens as he faces off with his first mate.

"And who was in charge of keeping her out of trouble?"

"I was, Captain."

Interested murmurs rise from the crowd around us,

and the man Will knocked out is starting to stir in the dirt at my feet.

"It's time to go."

Charles grabs my hand and tugs me along. "We have two more places to visit."

"She'll deliver?"

Will nods his head back towards the tavern we just left, and Charles nods in answer.

The next two appointments go down without incident, and I'm ready to fall asleep on my feet by the time the sounds of the waves against the docks fill the air again.

The only thing holding me up is Charles's long fingers clasped around mine. His hands grip around my waist as he lowers me into the boat.

I'm unsteady on my feet, and for one horrible second, I think I'm about to tip the boat.

But I don't, and the man who's been waiting in the little boat rows us back out to the Lady Monroe.

I close my eyes for a second, and Charles nudges me.

Did I fall asleep?

"Can you climb up the ladder?"

"Yes."

My voice must sound as tired as I feel, because he stays closely behind me the whole way up. Close enough to catch me if I miss my steps.

I breathe a sigh of relief once my feet are on the deck again.

I grip the railing with both hands while Charles and Will talk in low voices. I drop my head back to look at the stars twinkling down at me.

So steady and eternal. As if they've already seen all there is to see. As if they already know how this story will end.

I wish I knew too.

Or maybe it's better that I don't.

CHAPTER 21

Tress

A sparkly tapestry of blue and purple floats above the rigging. There are so many stars here. Even more than I see at Rocky Beach after dark.

Pain etches in my chest at the thought of home, of Eon.

Will I ever be at Rocky Beach again? Ever see my brother? Or Chris and John?

Charles wraps his arm around my shoulders, and tingles spread like lightning where the warmth of his body seeps through my garments.

"You look like you're dead on your feet. Come."

I follow him across the deck, to the doorway leading down below.

His hands are gentle as they steady me down the worn steps, and across the uneven plank floor, as he opens the door to his cabin.

A chill spreads in my stomach as I remember the anger that radiated off him outside the tavern. I hurt him, even if it was in accidental self-defense.

"Are you angry with me?"

My voice is weak, full of the fear that I can't tamp down.

He closes the door before answering, and I press a hand to my mouth.

I'm going to throw up.

Memories of raised voices and angry outbursts, and the closing of doors preceding them crowd my mind until I can't breathe, can't feel.

A tear slips down my cheek and words meant to exonerate me start to tumble out of my mouth.

"I was just trying to help the girl. She could have been me, and I needed to help her. Will wasn't going to, and I..."

Charles is beside me in the next moment. He pulls me into his arms. His voice is kind, his breath warm against my face.

"I'm not angry with you, Treasure. I know certain things are different in your time."

But not as different as one might hope. Not for young girls with no one to protect them.

"I was just like them once, and I couldn't stand by and watch when they needed me."

Strong arms tighten around me.

Safety blooms in my chest. My muscles slowly release the tension they've held for so long.

You're not in danger.

Not between the walls of this ship's cabin, not between the arms of this man.

His grip loosens enough that I can easily tip my head back and see the intent in his eyes. The tender expression on his face.

He's not going to hurt me.

Charles Seewell has proved himself nothing but trustworthy. I'd decided long ago that love is not for me. Neither is infatuation. But if ever I wanted to find it, deep in my bones I know he is the one I'd want to find it with.

If I wanted it.

But you do want to find love.

Fear makes blood pulse behind my eyes, hiding the man in front of me.

I drop my eyelids, fighting the impulse to run.

It's the heartache you don't want.

If I fall in love with Charles and he leaves too, isn't it just the final nail in the coffin? Proof to all and everyone that I'm unlovable?

My own parents couldn't be inspired to raise me or love me.

Don't parents naturally love their children? What did I do as an infant that was so horrible that they couldn't find a way to deal with parenthood?

Eon couldn't find enough love for me to fight his demons. He let them have all of him as he left me behind.

Jonah didn't care to stay once he really knew me.

Lucas didn't find me worth waiting for. Not when I had baggage that held me back.

Do I need further proof?

"Treasure."

My name is something sought after, and I am anything but. I'm nobody's treasure and everybody's trash.

Warm lips press to a tear I didn't know was tracking down my cheek.

"I will not leave you."

"Then don't."

The whimper is all I can get out.

It's late. I'm dead on my feet, and the weight of the last forty-eight hours makes it feel like each one of them has repeatedly brought me to the brink of insanity.

"You should get some sleep."

But I don't need sleep.

I need rest.

And suddenly I can't rest unless I know he's right here with me.

We're still anchored in the Newport harbor, the danger is not over.

"Please stay here. Please don't leave me."

His eyes meet mine, his dark pupils eclipses the gray of his irises almost completely. There are millions of questions in them that I can't answer tonight.

"I need to know you're here, safe."

"You want me to stay in my cabin. With you?"

Is that such a ridiculous request? It's already *his* cabin. He's allowed to stay in it. But I know what he's asking.

"Please?"

The frown between his brows deepens.

"There are no secrets on a ship, Treasure. All of my crew knows I stayed the night outside my cabin last night. They'll know tonight if I don't, too."

The laugh I let out is half a sob.

"You're worried about my reputation? I think that's the least of my worries."

He slides the backs of his fingers over my cheek.

Spirals of pleasure run through my nerve endings like wayward electricity.

I close my eyes.

"Just stay. I'm not asking for...anything else. Just your presence."

And maybe it's foolish of me to do so. But I don't think Charles will take advantage of the situation.

And if he does?

His arms drop from around me, and he steps back.

He turns to the door, and the drop of the bolt reverberates through the room.

No one is coming or going through that door tonight.

The creaking groans of the ship, the rushing wind beyond the hull, and the steady movement of the great water all around us fills the silence.

My mouth is dry as I watch Charles put his tricorn hat down on his desk.

I turn away from him and unlace my borrowed boots. I don't have much in the way of sleeping clothes.

As far as I remember from history books I've read, shirts were worn day and night by the poorer classes.

Another thing I remember? Showing up in an undershirt is the equivalent of showing up naked.

And I have no plans to give Charles the wrong idea.

Except, the stiff, wide pants he's given me are grimy from climbing in and out of boats and traversing through the filth of the harbor. They're not something I feel comfortable dragging into his bed.

Who knows how often they change the bedding around here?

Probably never.

I tug the trousers off and look down at myself. In my eyes the wrinkled shirt that reaches mid-calf is more than modest.

But in his?

I don't know.

I tug the blankets aside, slide into the bed, and tuck the covers to my chin.

I study the knots in the wood and try to close my ears to his movements.

The step of his boots.

The creak of the bed frame as he sits on the edge of the bed.

The tug he gives his laces, the stiff leather sliding off his feet.

The thunk of his boots against the floorboards.

The rustle of clothing.

My throat tightens, and I can't breathe. Is there too little air or too much?

"Treasure."

The pine knots swim before my eyes.

I hear the sigh he lets out even over the furious pumping of blood in my ears.

The mattress dips even more as he moves his full weight onto the bed.

I'm going to suffocate.

On this night.

In this damp ship's cabin, where the smell of musty waterlogged wood is all around me.

Groaning wood, rustling bedding, and Charles's voice repeating my name in my ears.

I'm going to suffocate with the question in his voice that I can't answer.

His arm slips under my neck, and he tugs me close.

My cheek rests against his chest. The fabric of his shirt is still wet from my tears from minutes ago.

But he does nothing but hold me.

He doesn't take advantage.

Doesn't see my nightshift for what it's not. He is just here...with me.

My breath slips over my lips in relief.

For once…

Someone stays.

CHAPTER 22

Charles

The ship's wood groans underneath me as I return from the dream world.

Whenever I sleep, I dream of Treasure. And sleep must be holding onto me still, because I feel her soft body crushed to mine. Small, and warm, and tucked into my side. And so real, as if I could reach out to touch her and she'd be warm underneath my hand.

I let the palm of my hand rest where her chest rises and falls peacefully in slumber. And against my skin, she's warm, alive.

Clarity rushes in.

She's really asleep, but I'm not.

I withdraw my hand as if the fabric of her borrowed shirt is about to burn a hole through my skin.

She's really here.

I look at Treasure. Her lips are parted, her lashes resting against her cheeks, the frown that so often mars her brow unseen.

She's still asleep. But for how long?

We're so entangled, I don't know if I can remove my limbs from around her, or hers from around me without waking her.

Last night she asked me to stay, and I did. Against my better judgement.

I shouldn't have let her tear-filled eyes convince me. Shouldn't have stayed in this cabin with her, and definitely not in my bed *with* her.

Not that where I stayed within the walls of my captain's cabin would make much difference as far as her reputation goes.

I shouldn't have shared a bed with her, but I can't find it in me to regret it.

Slowly, I extract myself from her arms and my bed.

She whimpers, and I still.

Her hand closes around mine, and she settles again.

"Please don't...leave me."

The words are slurred.

I watch her face for signs of wakefulness.

There are none.

I escape the bed and pull my clothes back on. When I sit back down to fasten my boots, she's still asleep.

And it's good that she is.

Because once she wakes up I have to confront her with what I've done.

How I've held her while she slept as if I have anything to offer her here. As if I have any intention of ever doing so again.

Treasure looks innocent curled up on her side under my blankets. But I know well that women can be as devious as men.

I'm no longer the lad that believed Sarah Monroe's false promises. And since the day she counted our vows to each other for nothing and married a blacksmith, I have had no loyalty to give any woman.

Not even this one.

And worse than the life I can't give her? I've taken hers away.

She's trapped in my time now, on a lowly pirate ship. With a crew of wanted men, men who, save for Will, will do nothing to protect her if something happens to me.

If last night was proof of anything, it was of how foreign my world is to her.

Her steel grip on my hand the whole time we were off the ship. Her ability to start a brawl outside a tavern in the few minutes I left her with my first mate.

She doesn't belong here, and yet she'll have to find a way to do so. Because I can't bring her back to her own time.

Had we still been in the waters near the Triangle of Spirits, I might have tried. But sailing my ship from safety and into waters she's unlikely to return from?

I might as well walk up to the governor's door and ask him to hang us himself.

I shake my head and give the figure in my bed one last look.

I have much to do in the hours before we set sail. The goods I arranged for delivery last night will need to be loaded. I'll need to keep Will out of trouble, and oversee the mending of the sails and several minor repairs to the Lady Monroe.

And then...

Then I'll have to tell her. That I'm not taking her home.

I knock on my cabin door hours later.

"Charles?"

Her voice is uneven.

"It's me."

I shove the key in the lock and push open the door.

Treasure sits one the bed, hair disheveled and eyes wary, but as I enter, she lets out a sigh of relief.

At the sight of me.

The something that shifted in my chest when I found her reading in the library on Sunday morning stirs again. Slowly, as if it's been dead to the world for too long and no longer remembers how to.

But I remember.

I remember opening my eyes in that guestroom, closing my fingers around the hand that tended me for weeks, kissing the lips that told me every lie I'd ever wanted to hear.

Touching the wooden cross marking her eternal resting place.

But those memories fade as Treasure whispers my name. As she rises from the bed and steps closer to me with eyes full of fear—and longing.

And I see Treasure instead of Sarah. I see her like I did the first time I laid eyes on her.

As she runs towards me and drops her book into the water at her feet, mouth agape.

I see the firm set of her shoulders as she talks her way out of my quarrel with the soldiers outside the library grounds.

As she perches at the edge of her seat, eyes wide as she listens to my stories.

The clear pleasure on her face as she watches me at the railing of her ferry.

My cabin comes back into focus, and Treasure is but steps away, full lips parted and a glimmer of hope in her eyes.

Her hopeful expression hits my gut like a shovelful of ice. Because in my memories she is back in her own world. But I don't know if she will ever be there again.

The Lady Monroe is no longer close to the Triangle of Spirits, and I cannot bring my ship and crew back into those waters. We escaped once, but there is no guarantee we will be that lucky a second time.

I cannot offer her any sort of safety. I can't think of any other way to keep her safe than to find her a place on land.

The widow who housed Will and me as boys, before we went to sea, still lived in the River Colony the last time we docked in Mistick. I can convince her to let

Treasure stay with her. And if I can't, my gold can. Treasure would be safer there than anywhere else.

As safe as she could hope to be in a time she's wholly unprepared for.

Treasure's eyes are on mine and I know the admiration in the blue depths will cease when I tell her of my plan.

She won't look at me as she does now, and I already feel the loss.

The longing in her eyes burn into me as I close the last of the distance between us, just as she raises up to press her lips to mine.

Her mouth on mine is heaven. The dried black slate that used to be my heart cracks open until pink flesh carves its way out.

Her hands slide up my chest and circle around the back of my neck.

There's nothing I wouldn't do for her in this moment. Nothing I wouldn't—

I am a liar.

The only thing she wants, to go home, is the same thing I can't do for her. Won't do for her. And her chance to go back ends with her stepping off this ship.

"What's wrong?"

She pulls away, as if the stiffening of my body has alerted her. She looks up at me, a question in her blue eyes.

I can't tell her here. Not after kissing her like this. I need a minute to find the words that I'm certain will make tears well in eyes that are now watching me with confusion.

"Come up on deck with me. I need to talk to you."

And break your heart.

CHAPTER 23

Tress

I once went swimming in the wake of a storm, too young to know the dangers of storm surges and rip currents. For a moment I'm pulled back into my memory.

Terror flashes through me, folds over me like a wave coming on too fast, too strong.

Pushed onto my knees, in the pebbled sand, saltwater in my nose and eyes.

Lungs burning.

Mouth gasping for air.

But it's not a sudden wave that's washing over me. It's the words of the man standing next to me.

"What do you mean you can't risk it?"

I spit the words out on a gasp.

As if I've really just been pulled under by a stray wave.

But I haven't, not physically.

The Captain of the Lady Monroe stands before me with eyes that are hardening rapidly to granite and a set of his mouth reminiscent of something even harder.

Can this be the same man whose soft lips melted against mine minutes ago?

The same man whose arms were so gentle around me through the night? That tightened only as I drifted off to sleep, when he pressed the softest kiss to my temple as my breathing evened out?

It was my last memory before I woke up alone this morning, and I can't align it with the immovable pirate captain standing in front of me.

I take a step away from him, as if another ten inches will make a difference in his harsh words.

But air doesn't flow properly through my airways and into my lungs.

Not when he stares me down like he is.

Please don't fail me too.

My memories of him are all so jarringly opposite of the unbendable man across from me.

The man I remember has always treated me with gentleness.

When I woke him on my porch floor and he was coiled for attack, but made no move against me.

When he stepped away from the creep propositioning, and let him go, just to make sure I was unhurt.

As he wrapped his arms around me when I dissolved into tears in my front room after.

On the ferry when he first kissed me.

When he carried me below deck the day we came here.

Last night.

Always tenderness.

Never this unyielding mask.

I look at him as if my eyes can guilt him into helping me, into choosing to rescue me.

Please choose me.

"It is too dangerous. The Triangle of Spirits spells certain demise for my crew and ship."

The Triangle of Spirits. The area of the Atlantic Ocean where the ordinary looking book on his desk down in his cabin somehow gathered magic enough to push him into my world.

The same book I so foolishly touched and let it send me back here too.

He's not going to choose me.

I see it in his stance, in the eyes that don't soften for a second as they take me in.

I pull my gaze away from the man in front of me, and look out towards the open sea.

I might not have asked him to bring me here, but didn't I really want this rugged pirate to pull me out of my loveless existence?

It's not something I'll ever admit out loud. Not to him, not to anyone. I'll deny it till my last breath, even on threat of the cat o'nine.

Under which I'll never be if he has anything to say about it.

Captain Charles Seewell is not the only one at fault for bringing me here.

Deep down I wanted my life to change. I even wanted to be where he was.

I'm so stupid.

I thought only about how much I wanted to escape my current life, not about what another life might mean.

I'm not cut out for eighteenth century seafaring, or for living in the middle of harrowing tales of men's lives ending at the gallows. Nor for caring so deeply for a man who might meet such an end.

Love.

The emotion that never ends well for me. And still it bubbles under my breast bone, so tender it's painful.

I don't want to love you.

I want to scream at him. I want to make him take me back. This isn't what I had in mind when I sat by the ocean and dreamed of a different life.

I wanted a life where I would feel loved and cherished. Where laughter and kisses didn't end with the shutting of a book.

I wanted a life where Eon returned to be the brother I remember. The one I loved with all my heart, the one who protected me with his body.

But if Eon returns now he won't find me waiting.

I pull in a sharp breath as the ache of that thought crushes my breastbone.

"There is a widow. In Mistick. She could take you in, help you get accustomed. I'd pay her well."

He adds on the last bit as if it isn't the most insulting.

"You want to pay some woman you know to babysit me?"

He lets out a deep sigh, frustration evident on his face. Frustration that I'm not jumping with glee at his offer?

"I'm trying to keep you safe."

I can't go back on my own. I need this ship and its captain to take me there. But my wishes don't matter to him. Charles holds all the power here. And I hold none.

"Is that where we're going now? Mistick?"

He nods.

Oh, the irony. The modern day town is less than ten minutes from my house, but my house won't be built for another 200 years.

He turns away from me and faces the ocean.

I want to yell at him. But despair chokes the angry words in my throat.

We stand silent by the railing—the only barrier between the planks of the deck and the bottomless deep.

The shouts of sailors and the squawks of seagulls, ropes and wood groaning as they move the great ship are all drowned out by the silence between us. No words can adequately fill it.

It's not a benign quiet, there's no content in standing here next to him.

The pause between us is like the waters surrounding the Lady Monroe—the surface is barely moving, but underneath it rages in the depths of the ocean.

He's planning on dropping me off like an unwanted bag of donations.

When I said I wanted a different life, I meant one where I was wanted. Not yet another life full of people wanting to discard me.

Hurt swirls in me, the pressure so violent I can barely breathe.

I failed at keeping love at bay. While I wasn't watching it made a home within me. And tied me close to this man who wants to leave me.

Charles watches the ocean while I watch him.

He towers over several of his crewmen, just like he towers over me. His bronzed skin is an even deeper red than it was at home, courtesy I'm sure, of the merciless sun beating down over him since he returned to his ship.

Has it really only been three weeks since I first laid eyes on this man?

The deck rolls as we begin to move, and I tilt.

Charles's hand settles on my arm to steady me.

Even in the middle of a fight he's ready to support me.

I want to push his arm away, but I don't want to fall on my butt on the deck in front of him—again. Not in the middle of this argument, so I let him keep me upright.

His touch is gentle, but in his eyes the gentleness is receding.

"I can't risk the souls of twenty-six men to bring you home. We barely made it out last time."

But he's forgetting one, because he'd be risking his

own too. But he has no plans to risk anything for me.

Least of all his life.

"And what exactly do you have to offer me here?"

His face shutters.

"Nothing. Only a new life in Mistick, at the Widow Ackley's house."

A home with a stranger, in a strange time. That is all he has to offer me.

Pain reaches through my ribcage, taking ahold of my core, wringing out the dry shell of my heart as if there's anything left for it to bleed.

I shouldn't be surprised. He might have stayed last night. But I've known for a long time that I'm not the kind of girl people stay for.

I'm the kind they leave.

Voices echo in my memories, every one of them a justification for leaving me behind. Every one of them a bleeding scab in my chest.

I never wanted kids.

I can't take it, Tress, you need to let me go.

I love you, but I'm not in love with you.

I can't wait around forever.

I'm always the one they leave.

CHAPTER 24

Tress

Can I help you, miss?"

A burly crewman takes his eyes off the heavy rope he's wrangling into a circle around his arm, and turns an annoyed look in my direction.

Heat spreads in my cheeks.

Was I staring? I must have been. In reality I was just lost in thought. Dreaming up a thousand happy dreams where Charles's words this morning don't take a deadly stab to my balloon of hope.

"Um no, I'm fine."

I mumble the words, my embarrassment growing proportionally with his irritation.

"Perhaps you'd like to go be fine on another part of the deck? You're unnerving me with your staring."

My cheeks burn hotter.

I've definitely been staring, then.

I have wondered how the Lady Monroe's crew really feels about me, but no one has made comments that I've heard. I thought perhaps that was because they were okay with my presence here.

By the leering stares from some of the crew, they've been more than okay with my presence here.

I shudder.

Perhaps it doesn't mean anything that they haven't aired their grievances around Charles. The scowl on this sailor's weathered face certainly makes me think so.

Tsking sounds to the right of me, and a heavy arm drops around my shoulders.

Not expecting it, the sound of disapproval or the arm, I jump.

"Aww, don't be such a naysayer, Mose. She doesn't mean no harm."

Will turns his wide grin on me and makes a show out of his next stage-whisper.

"He doesn't bite, he's just jealous he doesn't have *his* girl onboard."

Will's eyebrows waggle, and the scowl on the other sailor's face deepens.

Will's implication makes my ears burn, and I shrug out of his hold.

I don't want anyone to get the wrong idea about what I'm doing aboard this ship. Especially not after that easily misconstrued speech.

The breeze coming off the water is cool against my hot face.

It's my third day on the ship, and everyone but me is running around like busy worker bees, loading goods and making repairs. Well, everyone but me and Will.

I frown at him, not at all happy with his intrusion.

"Don't you have something more important you should be doing?"

A dimple flashes in Will's cheek. I doubt he suffers for female company when the Lady Monroe makes port. He's much too charming to spend much of his time alone.

"Alas, Captain has promised to keelhaul me if I don't keep an eye on you, so we'll hope the crewmen will carry their own load today."

There's a hint of irritation in his voice, almost drowned out by the sparkle in his blue eyes. Almost.

A gasp slips across my lips. I've done just enough reading to know how deadly keelhauling can be.

"He wouldn't really keelhaul you, would he?"

Amusement shines in Will's eyes. "Let's not find out, huh?"

"Have you been watching me the whole time?"

I remained at the railing after Charles left me here a while ago, and I'd been a little nervous at first. He's kept such a close guard on me since we arrived on the ship, going as far as to have a guard at my locked door, and he's never before left me alone on deck.

But apparently, I wasn't unguarded this time either.

I don't know how I feel about having a baby sitter. But as I survey the men that make up Charles's crew flitting to and from, I'm not so sure the feeling isn't relief.

None of them look to be the type of adversary you'd survive in a back-alley encounter.

Glints of weapons are everywhere—knives, swords, and muskets tucked into boots and belts. One man has a puckered, pink scar from his eye to his jaw, across his lips. The grin he gives me is deformed and unsettling. But not because of his scar. Another man is missing half his ear. Some of the scars I see around me are grislier than others, but not one of the crew is without one.

I look at Will and the scar that cuts his eyebrow in half. It's thin and white. Will still has his good looks, but for how long?

Probably not long. And the same probably goes for the man I'm trying my best not to think about.

I shudder, wanting to let the commotion on deck suck away any of my overthinking. Of course, that's too much to ask.

The rank smell coming off of several of the crew members whenever they pass too closely hints at a poor understanding of personal hygiene.

One man's eyes stay on me too long, and the smirk he gives me makes me shudder.

Suddenly I'm glad Charles has put Will on babysitting duty.

I lean against the tiny area of railing where no one seems to be doing anything right then and watch the bustling harbor.

It's oddly familiar, but not.

A bit like the eighteenth century seaport museum I grew up visiting, but brighter. The accents that float across the water are sharper, the smells stronger, and some not pleasant at all. There's not a single cargo-shorted tourist dad with a camera around his neck and a brood of children in sight.

I am so far from home.

"What's that sad face for?"

Will is at my side again. Morning sunlight flints off the gold earring in his ear.

Is it to pay his way to heaven with a proper funeral like I've read, or is it just jewelry?

Regardless, I think almost every man aboard has one.

How would I explain my predicament to Will? Can I?

I don't know what Charles has told him, but I remember how long he waited to tell me in my world, and his words from the beach.

"The story of how I made it to your library could have labelled me as in league with the devil where I come from."

I feel Will's eyes on me as he waits for my answer.

"I miss home."

"Aye, I guess that is bound to happen. Where is your home?"

I mention the town, and he nods.

To him it's not odd, I know my town was both founded and settled by this point in time. But I know we're also not remotely talking about the same place.

"Where are you from?"

He tells me. His pronunciation is different from mine, but then he's also almost 300 years before me. The thought makes the deck planks underneath me seem less substantial than they were a minute ago. I feel dizzy.

Apparently Will takes my silence for interest.

213

"I haven't been home since I was a lad. I met Captain Seewell, when we were both barely men, and I've been sailing with him since."

I slide my hand along the smooth wood of the railing. The wood is warm from the sun.

"How many years ago was that?"

His brow creases, and his eyes narrow for a moment.

"Sixteen or so?"

"Do you think you'll always be a sailor?"

Something shutters in his face, and I want to take my question back. Even more so when he speaks.

"I'm thinking most men in my position don't live long enough to think of *always*."

Facts I've read about this time period, referred to as the war on pirates, pop uninvited and unwanted into my mind. The average two years most pirates stayed alive in their trade. The gruesome punishments for those who were caught.

I hate that he's right.

Because his life expectancy is at worst the same, and at best a little better, than the man who makes my heart speed up whenever he's near.

I'm so angry with him I want to throttle him. But I don't really want him to die a gruesome death.

The thought of losing him makes me feel as if my heart is crashing onto sharp rocks of reality and horror.

Because I am losing him.

Whether I go home or he drops me off with his lady-friend I'm unlikely to ever see him again.

I still want to go home. Desperately. But suddenly I'm not so sure I want to be alone when I do.

The sky's glorious peach color bleeds into the pale blue evening sky as the sun sets. The pungent scent of salt-water and seaweed is all around me, and I can't help but close my eyes and breathe it in.

Awareness prickles on my skin, and my heart speeds up. A moment later, Charles moves to stand beside me.

I turn towards him, take in his bloodshot eyes and the weariness slumping his shoulders, and all I want to be is his rest.

To fold him into my arms and just listen to his heart. Feel his breathing even out.

Would he let me?

"Are we all set to sail?"

He sends me a look that I can't decipher, but he nods.

Above us the sails are already being unfurled from the yardarms. Those lazy summer days spent volunteering in the seaport left me with a few nautical terms, at least. Except the bona fide sailor who'd been showing us around had called them "big yellow sticks." Not such a nautical term, that.

"Where are we going?"

He stays quiet for so long that for a minute I think he's not going to answer.

"South."

I nod and look back out at the brilliant evening colors of the sky.

"You're not going to beg me to take you home?"

I look out across the water as the large planes of canvas above us stretches with the breeze, as if trying to catch it. They're loud.

"If you're asking if I still want to go home, the answer is yes."

"But?"

Captain Charles Seewell is still too observant for his own good, or in this case, mine.

Can I bare my heart to him?

The words I've read about the lifespan of a working pirate plays in my mind, joining together with Will's words from earlier.

"I'm thinking most men in my position don't live long enough to think of always.*"*

I still want to go home. But suddenly being centuries away from home and facing the possibility of losing the only person that makes me feel safe feels like too much.

"I just can't say I mind some more time with you."

The chuckle that follows my words is warm and spicy, like mulled cider and warmer touches.

I look up at him wanting to despise the smirk on his face, but I don't.

He's refusing to bring me home, dropping me like hot trash, and I should hate him.

I do hate him.

But I also love him.

Another press of his lips to mine can't change any of that.

And it won't change his mind about bringing me home, will it?

How wrong can it be to steal another kiss when, whether he brings me home or to the widow, I'll never see him again?

He hitches a hand around my hips and pulls me close. I have to tilt my head to look up at him.

His eyes are full of heat, but he hesitates, holding still instead of moving closer.

His eyes give me no clues about what he's thinking.

I almost pull away, but in the next second his lips are on mine, warm and all-consuming.

And I don't hate this at all.

My stomach drops with a delicious tingle as his other hand slides up my spine, making me arch into him.

I don't ever want to let go of the way I feel in this moment. If there were no more moments, I wouldn't care.

Because here, like this, I don't even want to go home. I don't want to be separated from him.

I want to stay right here as he presses me closer, as his mouth moves to my jaw, to my neck.

"I love you."

The words slip past my lips before they've processed in my brain, but Charles stiffens immediately. His mouth doesn't leave my skin, but his next kiss is nowhere near as heady.

And following it, instead of another touch of his mouth on my skin, he pulls away.

"What's wrong?"

"I have nothing to offer you here."

"Why? Because you don't want to, or because you are a pirate and one meeting with the law away from leaving me behind defenseless?"

"Yes."

My eyes burn. The regret over kissing him does the same.

What a foolish mistake that was.

Bitterness slips into my voice.

"You're refusing to send me home where I belong while also refusing to give us a chance here?"

But even as I say the words, I'm not so sure my own time *is* where I belong. It may be the only place I can survive on my own, but if Charles was by my side?

I let my heart dream for a second before he knocks me back down to the ground with his words.

"There is no us."

"How can you say that after what just happened?"

"That was a kiss. And it's the end and the beginning of what I have to offer you."

Tears spill over my cheeks at the callousness in his voice.

"Then take me home!"

219

"And risk the lives of twenty-six men for yours?"

I'm not worth that to him, of course I'm not.

The pain slices through muscle and bone deep into my core.

My brain understands that he can't risk his crewmen's lives for me, but my heart only feels like I'm the one he's willing to lose.

Again, I'm the one that takes the fall. The one who's not enough.

I'm never enough.

Love is not for you.

I wipe the tears from my face, but they only keep coming. They trail down my heated cheeks like rivers of melted pain.

When I walk away from him, no footsteps sound across the deck in pursuit of me. No voice calls my name, or asks me to be reasonable.

There's no reaction from him at all.

Because he doesn't care.

I love him. *I love him!* And he couldn't care less.

300 years in the past, history still repeats itself.

CHAPTER 25

Charles

Three days the water has moved around the hull of the Lady Monroe, since we harbored in Newport. Three sunsets and three sunrises, the waves of the deep and the wind pushing her sails have moved her forward.

We're no longer charting to reach the River Colony—there would be no way to lose a ship trying to overtake us, and that was what my lookout saw.

Treasure's hair blows in the same breeze that's kept our sails full. My hands ache to feel its softness under my hands again.

But I know she won't let me.

I don't even know if I would run the silky strands through my fingers if I had the chance.

I need to let her go.

Her slender fingers grip the smooth railing, and I long for her touch.

There is no mistaking the way the touch of her hand unravels me or how her smile lights places in my soul that have long been dark.

There's also no mistaking the three ships on the horizon, whose course has aligned with ours ever since we left our route to Mistick.

Treasure sighs as she leans her elbows onto the railing and lowers her chin to her clasped hands.

I take in the barely perceptible shadows on the horizon. The lookout spotted them hours into our voyage to Mistick, when we thought they were only passing merchant ships.

Not planning to attack any ships this close to Newport, and even less inclined to do so with the precious cargo we have on board, I paid them little mind.

In the hours that followed it was clear they were in pursuit, and I had to alter our course.

There would be no way to escape them so close to land. The open ocean was the safer bet.

I watch the woman who has brought impossible choices into my life.

Treasure wants me to return her to her own world, and until now, I've put the safety of my crew over her wish to return. But if these ships are really in pursuit?

She might get her wish yet.

I push down the desire to clamp my arms around her, watch her laugh with surprise, and cut the glorious sound short with my kiss.

But I do none of those things. Instead I speak her name.

"Treasure."

She turns to me, her expression wary. And she's right to be.

"What's wrong?"

She searches my face, and the fear in her eyes tugs at my heart.

I walk closer and point my finger towards the fate coming for us.

"See the dark spots out there?"

"Those shadows? What are they? Land?"

Oh, if only they were.

"They're ships."

"Oh. Is that good or bad? Are you going to attack them?"

The last question is tacked on, as if she's suddenly remembered what I do for a living.

"No, I'm not going to attack them. Not with you on board. But they might be planning to attack us."

Her eyes widen, and she turns back to the horizon.

"But they're far away, right? Wait, how many are there?"

"The lookout can see three."

"Three against one. Is that… Can you beat that?"

"On a good day, maybe."

No.

"Can we outrun them? What are we going to do?"

We. As if she's already resigned herself to a place next to me.

She might have. But I haven't.

Because next to me is a place she'll more than likely end up dead. Or worse.

"I don't know what I'm going to do yet."

But it's a lie.

"Captain."

Will nods his head towards the three ships that are now clearly outlined between us and the horizon.

I shoot another glance toward the woman I left standing at the railing. Dressed in men's clothing, she could almost pass for a young sailor. But she's so far from that.

My chest tightens.

"Keep an eye on her, Will."

Will groans.

"I'm at the wheel, Captain."

"Have Mose take a turn."

I nod to the burly crewman ambling across the main deck.

"Yes, Captain."

I turn my back on the exasperation in his voice. Will Hayes has been my first mate as long as I have been a captain. I know he'll obey my order regardless of how he feels about it.

The salty breeze whips around me as I move down the steps from the quarter deck. I cast another look at Treasure, and duck under the low beam and below deck to my cabin.

Crossing the room, I find the map I need. Spread out across my desk, I search for the three lines off the coast of the colonies.

And the skull next to them signifying certain death.

I trail my fingers across the faded lines of the parchment.

The Triangle of Spirits.

Cursed waters from which few sailing ships ever return.

The skull is the same as that on the flag we fly when in pursuit of other ships. But this time it's not we who are in pursuit.

And if the ships that have been gaining on us all morning know the Lady Monroe's trade, they won't let us go. Pirate ships carry both treasure and weapons, and whether it's a navy ship, privateers, or other pirate ships will make no difference. They will all be hungry for the riches found aboard.

I move the weights and the worn hide curls in on itself, as if it knows the plan that unfurls in my mind.

I close the door to my cabin and Will steps down from the main deck. He stops at my side, and fear clutches the heart that now beats fervently in my chest.

I growl.

"I told you to keep an eye on her!"

"Mose is at the wheel, and David is with her."

"You think a cabin boy can protect her against any of the crewmen aboard?"

My glare would make any other of my men cower. Not Will.

"With his life. And you need to know the ships are gaining on us. We can lose them if we go Southeast. We can cross to—"

"We're not. We're heading back towards the Triangle."

His face pales, and there's a thousand reproaches in his next word.

"Charles."

It's the name he never calls me. The one no one ever calls me but her.

"To bring her back?"

But he doesn't need to phrase it as a question. He already knows.

His eyes narrow.

"And if it loses us the chance of escape?"

"Then we fight."

"I didn't know you had a death wish, Captain Seewell."

"I don't."

I have a life wish. For her.

"I need her to live."

Even in the perpetual twilight below deck I see the moment his expression shifts from confusion to determination, and his lip curls. It's a smirk that has defied death more times than I can count.

"Then, let's go bring her home."

The plan is almost certain to lead to a watery grave.

But Will's arm wraps around my shoulder. Just like it did sixteen years ago. The hand that squeezes my shoulder now belongs to a man, not a boy. But his words are the same as then.

"After you, Captain."

And this time I *am* the captain, and not the cabin boy with a near unattainable dream.

But even a captain can entertain a hopeless dream, and as I step back onto the sunny deck I see mine.

I've sailed across the world in search of gold and gems, but now the only treasure I covet turns to look at me.

I take a moment to just watch her. Her hair whips around a rosy face with a tan she didn't have when I met her. Another thing she didn't have then?

The sparkle in her eyes. She's looked more alive here aboard my ship than I ever saw her in her own world.

And still I'll send her back there.

Because it's where she belongs.

CHAPTER 26

Charles

Low clouds form in front of us as the Lady Monroe rides the waves toward a place I never thought I'd willingly seek out. The dark mass of clouds and flashes of lighting should make me adjust my course.

But I won't.

Ropes strain and wood groans as my ship moves at a steady clip.

Canvas flaps ominously above me and I ignore the muttering of the men working my orders.

Behind us, gaining by the hour, are three ships. They don't carry the King's flag, but it doesn't mean they won't hunt us down like dogs.

My fists tighten on the silken wood handles of the wheel as a cloud shuts the last of the sunlight out, and darkness settles over the ship.

"Think we're close enough?"

Will is next to me, keeping an eye on Treasure and waiting to take over the wheel so I can send her home. I dip my head in answer, and Will's fingers wrap around the handle next to mine.

"Keep her steady."

"Yes, Captain."

I turn, and my boots carry me down the steps to the main deck. I stride across the deck planks toward her, and no longer hear the roaring wind in my ears, nor do I taste the salt on my lips.

I see only her.

Blood pounds in my ears.

If I ever doubted that Treasure was anything more to me than Sarah was, that doubt has been carried away on the wind of this moment.

The woman I will never forget turns to me. She leans against the railing at her back, and I want to do anything but what I'm about to.

Face tilted up to me, her gaze burns into mine. Fiery temptation licks my temples. It's all I can do to stand my ground.

For years I swore never again to let eyes like Sarah's trick me into sacrifice or loyalty. But Treasure's eyes are not Sarah's. And this time my sacrifice will bring life, not death.

I have loyalty to give this woman. And I will give it, whether she likes it or not.

And she won't like it.

Without stopping I bend to pick her up. Her squeal rings across the ship. If there was any doubt she wasn't a crewman, there's none now.

I cradle her against my chest, and there are a million other reasons I'd rather be carrying her down to my cabin like this. The hollers and hoots from my crewmen tell me they're thinking along the same lines.

I glance down at her blushing face as I ease us through the doorway to below deck.

Darkness wraps around us as I carry her down the steps. Just like I did her first day aboard. But this time she's not soaked and shivering.

I make quick work of the distance, and we enter my captain's cabin a moment later.

"What are you doing, Charles?"

There's laughter in her voice, and something else I can't discern.

I haven't pulled Treasure Hayden down to my cabin to spend time alone with her like my crew thinks. I've brought her down here to make sure she leaves.

I slide the bolt into place behind us, and set Treasure down on the floor in the half-dark of my cabin, holding her gaze for another second. One more of her looking at me as if I'm the answer to all her questions.

But I'm not.

The book on my desk is. The one that will bring her home as soon as we're close enough to the magic within the Triangle of Spirits.

"Do you know where we are?"

She shakes her head, a frown on her face. She looks from the bolted door and back to my face.

"We're close to the Triangle of Spirits."

Her brow smooths, and her lips part in surprise.

"You're taking me home? But I thought you said it was too risky?"

"I'm sending you home like you wanted."

My voice is gruff. It barely pushes the words out past my lips.

I see the moment she understands what I'm offering her. It's the same moment her eyes begin to dance with excitement.

Eyes as blue as the ocean on a cloudless day.

A moment later a brilliant smile blooms on her face.

And it's directed at me.

I feel it straight to the core of my being.

"What made you change your mind?"

"Remember the ships I showed you? They are in pursuit and likely looking to attack."

This makes her smile fall a little.

"But you can fight them off, right?"

"I'd rather not with you on board."

"Why are they attacking you? I thought other ships usually stayed away from pirate ships?"

"And pass up already collected treasure? Most pirate ships carry gold and riches from raids."

And this ship does too. But the only treasure on board I care about is the one who's frowning in front of me.

Her chin drops and she takes a step back.

"And your crew can beat three ships?"

I don't answer. There's no need to. From the look in her eyes, she already knows.

"So after I leave, what will happen to you?"

"Does it matter? You won't see me again in your world."

Her mouth drops open in shock, but I refuse to take back my words.

I should never have let her close.

I close my eyes and in my memories Sarah's eyes well with tears like Treasure's will any minute.

But no.

When I open my eyes, a tear-filled gaze isn't what meets me.

Treasure's eyes spark with anger. She jabs my chest with her finger, pushing me back a step.

"And you wouldn't even consider coming back with me? Not even when your life is in danger? Do you despise me that much?"

I harden my voice.

"It's what I want."

The lie slithers through my chest, poisoning the heart that pounds against my ribs. My chest rises and falls as if I'm in the midst of a battle.

And I am.

"I love you!"

She spits the words at me, but I see the hurt behind the anger in her eyes.

She may think I'm the only one for her now, but she'll bind herself to another man some day as surely as Sarah did.

Maybe even as fast.

The venom from that thought slides into my next words.

"You may think you love me, but you don't. You'll go back to your own world and find someone else. I don't want you."

The lie falls off my lips without effort.

Her sharp intake of breath tells me my words hit the intended target. But the pain in her eyes brings me no pleasure.

Her hand drops, and she steps close to me, until we're chest to chest. The fire in her eyes pierce me again, and though I know she's trying to persuade me, she's doing the opposite.

"You think this isn't real?"

She presses her soft lips to mine, and every ragged piece of heart left in my chest settles.

Her warm hands slide like silk against my bearded jaw, her fingertips against my neck. Her fingers curl in my hair and she never takes her mouth off mine.

The pull of her fists and the softness of her mouth threatens to undo me.

When she pulls away, the weight beating in my chest is too heavy. Too much for my years of discipline to contend with.

Our seconds together have a final count now, they are measured out and dwindling fast.

But for this moment, this glorious space in time, she is mine.

"Come back with me. Please."

I wrap my arm around her torso, pulling her back to me with a force that makes her eyes widen. A yelp falls from her lips.

I only pause long enough for a triumphant smile to surface on her face, then the crinkling corners of her eyes sing to me, and I'm lost to her spell.

I kiss her with a desperation I've never known before.

Not with Sarah.

Nor any woman before or after her.

Not even when Sarah was lost to me, and then to the world, did my body inhabit this intensity of feeling.

Treasure Hayden is my home. My very soul calls to hers. This woman is my last tether to sanity. To life. To love.

And it leaves no doubt in my mind.

I have to let her go.

CHAPTER 27

Tress

When he finally moves his lips from mine, the room spins around me.

I want more, so much more. And I never want him to stop.

I lean towards him, eager to claim all that is mine.

"Again."

But he pulls away, and shakes his head. Still breathing hard from our kiss, the curse he lets out is disjointed and breathy, but I know it for what it is.

Understanding settles like ice in my stomach. His face doesn't display the features of a man who has come to his senses.

He still wants to send me away and stay behind to face the music without me.

I want to go home.

But without him?

He rubs his hands over his face, and I want to scream at the exasperated look he sends me. As if I'm a child that doesn't understand, can't understand, that this is the only course of action.

But it isn't.

It can't be.

Going almost 300 years back in time might have seemed a mistake at first, but I know now that although this is the past, the man in front of me is my future.

"Come with me, Charles. Or let me stay."

He groans.

"Treasure, there is a battle coming for me. We might have been certain of victory in favorable weather and calm waters. But this close to the Triangle of Spirits? It's far from certain. And if they board this ship and find you—"

His lips clamp together over the words he was about to say, as if he's not willing to even speak aloud the atrocities he knows might come my way. *Will* come my way if his crew doesn't win this battle.

He's right, I know he's right.

But leaving now means never seeing him again. And I can't handle that.

I won't survive one more goodbye. I have reached my

limit of goodbyes. Had reached it before I met him.

"Then you'll have to win the battle."

I know every man on board is a skilled fighter. There's no way to survive pirate-life for as long as they have without skill or obscene amounts of luck. And most likely both.

I am not blind, the impenetrable, billowing blackness I saw on the horizon before Charles dragged me below was as terrifying to me as the clearly visible ships I could make out behind us. The ships in pursuit of the Lady Monroe.

Still, I can't believe it. The man standing in front of me now is nothing like the man who mere days ago refused to even think about sailing into these waters to return me home.

"It is too dangerous. The Triangle of Spirits spells certain demise for my crew and ship."

I begged him, and still he held his ground.

And now he's willingly sailing into the same waters of death, pursued by at least three ships.

I don't see a way out of this for him, or his crew.

Instead of charting a course into waters where he'd have some advantage, he's sailing into certain death.

I'm so angry I could scream at him, but I don't. Instead

239

I nail him with a withering glare that has no effect on him whatsoever.

"You need to go back now, Treasure."

There is no question in his voice. He isn't asking me. He's just decided how I need to live my life.

"What makes you think you get to choose for me?"

"What makes you think it's a choice?"

His voice is gruff and his eyes bloodshot.

My heart wants to relent. I see the pain it's causing him, but I won't give in. Not on this.

"Please, Charles, come with me. I won't be able to return if I go."

I curse the tremor I hear in my voice. But I'll beg him if I have to.

"I don't want you to return. I want you to go. I want you gone."

I gasp, as if the dagger to my heart is physical. The way my breastbone radiates pain, I worry for a second that it is.

"You don't mean that."

"I mean it."

The man who kissed me as if he couldn't get enough of me is gone. And in his place is a man who wants me gone forever.

I won't cry.

I step backward and stumble.

After a week at sea I've more than gained my sea legs, and the movements of the ship in calm waters don't easily tip me. But these aren't calm waters.

Not this close to the Triangle.

Charles's arm shoots out to steady me just as a howl sounds from outside the ship. The vessel rocks, the force of the waves stronger than just seconds ago.

Which means that we are close to the cursed waters that first brought him to me.

The same ones he wants to use to push me away.

Forever.

His strong fingers grip my forearm as another gust of wind shakes the ship.

"Tress. I need you to leave. Now."

He's only ever called me Treasure, and the name he's never called me feels like a slap.

The wind whines outside the walls of the cabin, rocking the ship.

I shiver at the sounds coming from outside. If I stay, I'm in for a terrible storm, and a possibly worse battle.

For a second I wonder if he's right.

But of course he's not.

I shake my head.

"Put your hand down on the book."

"I won't."

He stares at me for a long beat, eyes softening for just a second before they turn hard again.

Is he going to relent?

Gray light spills into the cabin, as if the cloud cover is still letting through a little daylight, and I see the determination in his eyes.

"Please don't leave me."

I am begging now.

"Please don't leave me, too."

Charles's arms close around me, and he pulls me off my feet. He tucks me against his chest where his heart pounds as fast as mine.

For a moment I think he's finally seen reason. I'm suspended in the air, held firmly between his arms.

The only place I ever want to be.

I touch my hand to his stubbled jaw, wanting to pull him into a kiss.

Then he sets me down on his desk.

On top of the cursed book.

Magic prickles through my body, sparking in my fingertips. I try to vault myself off the desk, but his hands are holding me too firmly.

He's too strong.

The words I scream at him are as untrue as they are cruel, but water is already filling my mouth, cutting them off.

Then...

I can't feel his arms, can't hear his voice saying my name.

Dark water pushes everything else away. The cabin, the desk. The book.

My consciousness.

And the last thought that zips through my brain slices my heart open.

He's gone.

CHAPTER 28

Charles

She's gone.

I touch the place where she just sat, but my fingers brush nothing.

Not even the book.

There's no visible evidence of her ever being here.

The scent of her hair, her skin, still clings to the air in front of me. But for how much longer?

Pain springs up in my chest. I labor to take a single breath without her here.

The space closes around me, the walls of the cabin shrink until they are pushing against my chest from every side, strangling the breath in my throat.

Her hateful words still sting.

But I had no choice.

She needed to go back.

I needed her safe. Needed to know the men on the ships overtaking us would never be able to put their filthy hands on her. Never hurt her.

I draw in the last breath of air I shared with her, and then I turn my back on the place where she was, knowing I'll likely never have the reminder of it.

Not after this battle.

I step back onto the main deck into a sheet of rain. A wave washes across the deck. I grab the doorway to keep it from sweeping me overboard as the ship tilts.

Thunder cracks the sky above us and a flash of lighting washes everything in a bright white light.

"Will!"

I roar his name as the ship careens to the starboard side.

I'm on the quarter deck a moment later, and something makes a splash on the port side.

"Just keeping her afloat, Captain. We're under fire."

The boom of thunder covered up the noise of the first cannon, but the second bellows through the air.

"Ready the cannons!"

"Already done, Captain. You can give the order to fire."

I do, just as another cannon ball sails through the air over the bowsprit. A fountain of water rises up where it hits the water on the other side.

Men holler as their voices crack under the force of their yells. The Lady Monroe shakes as our cannons boom. Spears of fire light up the night as we unleash our deadly load.

The shrieks on impact tells we struck the deck we aimed for.

"Great shot, McDilly."

The sharp scent of gunpowder hits my nose. Grunts and shouts fill the air. A splash tells me the ship firing back at us missed their shot.

I move from the gun deck up to the quarter deck where Will is still at the helm. His wild grin tells me that this is what he was made for.

Some men would let terror overcome them in the face of three armed ships surrounding their vessel. Not Will.

"Watch, we're going to hit the stern."

He points and his grin widens.

The cannonball splinters the wood of the stern on the other ship, and Will hoots. It's not a hit they'll easily recover from. But they are but one ship.

I take the wheel from Will, and my thoughts leave the battle going on around me.

Her laugh echoes in my ears, not from beyond the grave, but through time.

The feel of the wheel against my palms fades and I can almost feel her soft hands curl around mine. Can almost feel the way the sparkle in her eyes jolts my heart into beating.

A crewman lets out a yelp and then a string of curses at my side.

"Musket fire!"

My voice grows hoarse as I shout orders above the din of the battle.

"Will! McDilly!"

"I'm on it, Captain!"

"Yes, Captain."

A bullet narrowly misses Will's shoulder as he leaps over the steps from the quarter deck and sprints across the main deck.

The noise of the battle fades around me, and in place of it, I see her.

Treasure Hayden's presence in my life these last few weeks was supposed to have no lasting impact.

But she does.

Her shadow taunts me. Even in the midst of battle, where no physical thing should remind me of her.

A boom tries to pull me from the vision of her as another cannon fires off, its flames coloring the air orange for a moment.

Cheers rise from the deck as our cannons hit the mast of the ship closest to the Lady Monroe.

Howls of men mortally wounded part the air, but it all comes to me as through a veil.

Her memory won't let me go.

Sending her back was the right thing to do, wasn't it?

Surely the book that tore me from my ship into her library had nothing to do with her?

When the magic returned me to my own world, her passage next to me was an accident.

Or was it not?

The ship thuds with the impact of another ball of iron, and I steady myself as my mind spins.

"Hooks!"

Will's voice penetrates the fog in my brain, and I see grappling hooks digging into the railing like claws.

"Cut the ropes! Now!"

Will obeys my order before I give it. He cuts one, then a second.

Another crewman drives his cutlass through the ropes of a third grappling hook, but the fourth hits him with a force that topples him over. His screams tear through the air.

More men crowd him, cutting ropes as they come.

Treasure found the book, not I.

It was *her* the book pushed through the barrier of time.

Not me.

Was the book meant for her all along?

"Captain!"

Will's shout has me turning just as a cannonball caves in the planks of the deck next to me. Too close to the wheel.

I let out a curse and Will joins me as his sprint brings him close enough to survey the damage.

They didn't hit the wheel, but their next shot might.

Will sends me a look, and he doesn't need to voice the thought in both our minds.

If their next shot hits its target, none of us will survive this battle.

It is why I sent Treasure away.

To keep her safe. Even if it meant never laying eyes on her again. Never feeling her soft skin under my hands, or her lips against mine.

I had no loyalty for a woman—until her.

But as I watch the dark hole in the deck planks, while the night is lit up by fire from cannons yet again, I doubt my actions.

"Tell them to keep firing into the hull. She's too close."

Will nods and disappears into the melee of crewmen and powder smoke. The next moments will make it clear who will win this battle.

Did I prove my loyalty to Treasure by sending her away when everything in me wanted to keep her close to me?

Is that how she sees it from where she is?

Or did I do exactly the opposite of what I intended—what every man before me has done?

Did I push her away?

Abandon her when she needed me the most?

If the sounds of fighting men and screams of agony doesn't make it clear, the sudden burning in my side does.

Fiery pain licks at my insides and the dark stain that spreads on my white linen shirt affirms it—whether I've let her down, or given her my love the only way I can...

I'll never know.

CHAPTER 29

Tress

The rug underneath my cheek is soaked with seawater. It's sticky and gross against my skin, and the rank stench of seaweed turns my stomach.

I don't have to look around to know where I am. There are no rugs like this one in Charles's captain's cabin. And if there were, I wouldn't be lying face down on it without him.

Without him.

Sorrow burns in my chest.

I twist my head around, so my eyes can tell me what I already know.

I'm alone.

More alone than I've ever been.

The nausea overpowers me.

Running footsteps sound as I dry heave.

"Tress! Oh my word. What happened to you?"

Chris kneels next to me, her pristine black pants immediately soak through at the knees from the puddle of water around me.

She pulls my hair to the side, and I can see more than her knees.

"What on earth happened?"

She tries to help me to my feet, but my legs wobble, and she's not strong enough.

"John!"

I frown at her yell.

Why would John be here?

"Hey babe, what?"

He's next to me in another second, easing my arm over his shoulder, and as long as John is holding me up, it doesn't seem to matter that my legs won't hold my weight.

"Ladies room."

I let them bring me into the bathroom, let Chris wipe my face and mouth with wet paper towels.

I barely feel the coolness against my numb skin.

"Why are you wearing these clothes? And how did you get so wet?"

I shake my head.

It doesn't matter.

"Does this have anything to do with Charles?"

But I can't tell her, can't form the words to tell her that he's gone.

He's gone.

I burst into tears.

"Oh darling, I'm so sorry."

She wraps her arms around my shoulders and pulls me close to her. Rocking me back and forth as if I'm a small child.

"I'm going to kill him."

John lets out a string of swear words, and for the first time in as long as I can remember, Chris doesn't hush him in my presence.

As furious as John is on my behalf, Charles will be safe enough.

He's left me to fend for myself, just like every other man before him.

He was supposed to prove me wrong. But he didn't. He proved me right by pushing me away. Out of his life. Forever.

He's gone.

Just like I knew he'd be.

Chris rubs her hand up and down my back, then repeats the motion on both my upper arms.

"Honey, you're shivering. Why don't you let me bring you home. I'll have Anja cover for us."

She pats my cheek, not seeming to expect an answer.

"John, help me get her out to the car, and I'll ask Anja to come in early."

I'm curled up in the passenger seat of John's truck. It smells like new leather and the salt water drying on my clothes.

"Tress, what happened to you?"

I shake my head as my eyes well with tears again.

"Are you hurt? Did he hurt you?"

I shake my head again.

It's a lie, but not to John's real question. He's asking for external bruises, intentional abuse. What I have is a broken heart. Not as illegal. Nothing he can run by his friends at the station. Charles doesn't have a record if he were to try.

"He doesn't have a key to your house, does he? If you need me to change your locks, I will. Just say the word."

"He never had a key."

Chris opens the car door and seats herself in the back seat.

"Do you want to go home, or to our place?"

"Home, please."

I don't want to go home at all. Not when so much of my apartment has memories of him. Not when it's the place I am the most alone.

But my clothes are there and the cold is starting to seep into my bones.

An hour later I am clean and dry, sipping hot chicken soup that Chris has somehow assembled from the meager contents of my fridge.

I suspect John ran out to the store while I showered, because I know I didn't have chicken.

But as my body recovers, my heart does not.

The mug in my hand is the one Charles drank coffee from the morning he woke up here. I consider asking Chris for another, but the memory of his hands around it warms me in a way the soup can't. I wrap my cold fingers around the mug, and press it to my cheek.

I miss you so much.

As if he's still within reach.

I bury my nose into the folds of fuzzy blanket around me.

I once let a stranger use it when he insisted on sleeping on my porch floor. It still smells faintly of salt and leather.

Of Charles.

Chris enters the kitchen doorway. Her red nails wrap around the side of the frame, and her eyes on me are intense. As if she's trying to look through to my soul to find out what happened. Why she found me soaked in seawater in the library basement, wearing clothes from a different era and many sizes too big.

But what could I tell her?

The truth would only make her worry for my sanity.

"Did you do the dishes?"

"I made a bit of a mess cooking up the soup."

Her red lips tilt up at the corners, but the worry stays in her eyes.

"It's not my business, and you can tell me to mind my own, but... Did you and Charles break up?"

Were we even together?

But if we were, we aren't anymore. I know that for sure.

"I think so."

Pain etches into my chest at the words, at the place where I left him.

Is he even alive anymore?

His words ring in my ears.

"There is a battle coming for me. We might have been certain of victory in favorable weather and calm waters. But this close to the Triangle of Spirits? It's far from certain."

He might be dead for all I know.

Tears well in my eyes, and sobs shake my shoulders.

"Oh, sweetie. I didn't mean to upset you. Why don't you let me stay here tonight? I'm worried about you."

Chris stays the night, after John hauls an air mattress into my house and fills it up. But as darkness settles outside my window, sleep won't come.

The bed is too soft, and too still. The sound of waves against the hull absent.

I can't sleep, and I wonder if I ever will.

CHAPTER 30

Tress

It's been seven excruciating days since I last saw him. Seven days since I screamed at him, and left him to certain death.

I asked for a week off work, and tomorrow I'm supposed to go back.

But I am not ready.

Not by a long shot.

I picture again the determination on his face. Feel his arms hauling me up against him, holding me up as if I was no burden at all.

I close my eyes and feel the sharp pricks of his stubble against the pads of my fingers. As if he's right here next to me.

The scents of leather and seawater and him fills my nose and euphoria my chest.

But when I open my eyes, I only see my empty living room surrounding me.

He is not here.

My phone pings with a notification, but just like Chris's numerous texts, it goes unanswered.

I read the first few she sent.

"I asked John to drop off some dinner for you. It should be on your porch."

"Anja asked after you today, I wasn't sure what to tell her."

"How are you feeling?"

The truth is that I don't. Instead, numbness seems to seep through everything that once made me feel alive. I don't feel sad. I just don't feel.

As if there's just a gaping blackness where my heart used to be. As if my soul has forgotten how to be—apart from him.

I put my tattered copy of *Persuasion* back down on the couch. My favorite book doesn't light up my insides anymore. It does nothing for me, other than remind me of my loss.

As Anne Elliot is abandoned by everyone she loves, in body and spirit, her heartache only intensifies my own. And when her captain returns, and mine is still absent, it brings me no joy.

Instead it makes me want to vomit.

I pick the book back up and launch it at the other end of the couch. I press my hands against my lips to quiet the strangled sob that tears from the bottom of my soul.

How did I used to think that the love I found in books was enough? That the loyalty of friends in stories could keep my tattered soul together? That trusting in their fictional love was enough?

How did I never feel the raging emptiness of this moment? Of every moment since Charles's hands faded from around my waist?

I bury my face in my hands again.

How did I never notice how lifeless the letters lined up, page after page into infinity?

Did I really think that fiction was a replacement for lived life?

Now the scent of ink fades in the memory of that of wood saturated with years of saltwater.

The feel of paper falls flat in the face of the calloused hand resting against the back of my neck in my memories, his fingers that send sparks like jolts through my nervous system with every brush against my tender flesh.

The scenes from my days at sea, my days with him— brimming with smell, and taste, and touch—are cemented in my memory, far more colorful than any I've read in books.

I close my eyes trying to still the stream of memories. But it won't shut off. It won't stop.

I open my eyes and jump up from the couch. Dizziness blurs the edges of the room for a moment.

I need to eat. I know I do. But everything I push past my lips tastes like sand in my mouth. My favorite dishes as palatable as ashes.

Nausea is now my constant companion, and though my cramping abdomen protests wildly, a grown woman can, it turns out live only on tea with cream and sugar. At least for seven days.

My phone vibrates on the coffee table. A string of vibrations buzz through the air as the green call icon lights up the screen.

Chris.

I watch the phone scoot closer to the edge of the coffee table with each vibration, until it topples over the edge.

That makes two of us.

But the phone lands softly on the rug. Unlike my own landing on the soaked basement floor in the library.

The ringing stops.

For a blessed minute the room is still. Then it starts again.

I groan and bend over to pick it up.

"Chris?"

"So you are alive?"

The sarcasm in her voice doesn't cover the relief coating it.

I roll my eyes even though she can't see me. "Unfortunately."

"Sweetie, that's not something to joke about. And you're not alone."

I don't answer. Because what is there to say?

Charles Seewell leaving was inevitable. And without him I am alone. Achingly, excruciatingly alone.

"John and I are here for you. I wish you'd tell us what happened..."

If I could without having my mental faculties doubted, I would. But the story I remember is too wild, too...

Charles's words from the beach sound in my head again.

"But you didn't believe it more than a drunkard's delusions, did you?"

My sob breaks into Chris's monologue. I can't stop the ragged grief that pushes up through my throat.

Grief for a man I never wanted to fall in love with, but that I did.

"Oh, Tress. I'll be over soon."

And within the hour she is at my door. Offering freshly baked bread. Moving around my kitchen as if she has all her life. Putting the kettle on and pouring mugs of tea.

"Why don't we sit down on the couch and you can tell me what happened?"

"It hurts so much to keep it all inside."

I wrap my hands around my mug and eye the couch as if it might swallow me up if I take a seat next to Chris.

"Then tell me. You don't have to carry this alone. Whatever it is, I'll listen without judgement."

"You won't believe me. *I* barely believe it."

"Try me."

The tilt of her red lips reminds me of Will's, and my heart smarts again.

I tell her. About Will, and Charles, and the Lady Monroe. Of the girls outside the tavern, and of the Triangle of Spirits.

Her eyes behind the cat eye glasses are soft with compassion as my words tumble over each other on their way out of my mouth.

Her shoulder with the pristinely black cardigan is soon stained by my tears.

But all my tears change nothing. The words I mumble and the half-cocked story that is mine to tell changes nothing.

Charles is still gone.

He is still gone.

CHAPTER 31

Charles

*S*he will never forgive me for abandoning her.

My body bobs up and down in water that slowly numbs my lower half, and I know it's the truth.

I abandoned her when she needed me. The one thing she begged me not to, and still I didn't listen.

"Please don't leave me."

Treasure's voice echoes through my mind. The vulnerability in her eyes plastered to the inside of my eyelids.

I can still hear the pain in her voice, feel the desperation in her touch.

And still I sent her back to her own world.

She will never understand that I had no choice. Not a real choice. Not when sending her back meant I could keep her safe.

And I needed to keep her safe.

Water laps at the piece of wood keeping me afloat in the freezing water. The air is heavy with gunpowder smoke. Echoes of death drown out the noise of the living.

My eyes linger on the burning remnants of my Lady Monroe. The proud vessel that carried my crew of pirates across the mighty sea for five years. That safely brought us through squalls and battles at sea alike.

Soon she'll be in the depths of that same ocean.

Flames lick at her once strong timber, lighting the night with its orange glow. Illuminating the burnt and blackened canvas that is all that is left of her sails.

The proud Lady Monroe bobs in the water, a damaged hull emptied of her treasure. Her crew died protecting her, and her captain will follow them soon.

By morning, all that will be known of her will be a heap of charred driftwood carried on the waves.

I pull in a shallow breath. Pain pierces my side. Again. But duller this time. Soon, I will no longer feel it.

We fought well. The Lady Monroe is not the only ship reduced to rubble.

But fighting well does not equal victory, nor does it negate the loss of good men. Men I couldn't leave to face this battle alone.

Sorrow stirs in my chest as Will's face fills my memories.

"After you, Captain."

I remember the words in the voice of the boy who stepped next to me up the gangplank of the European, off the solid ground we'd both walked all our lives. The lanky arm he threw over my shoulder and the smirk on his freckled face. The boy who would grow into my first mate. Who would die for my Treasure.

I last saw Will in combat, holding his own against a skilled fighter, moments before a cannonball blasted to pieces the deck planks between us.

The first nail in the coffin for the Lady Monroe, and the last I saw of my friend.

The smoke didn't lift after that blow. Another blast shook the ship and as men fled for their lives, others remained lifeless where they fell.

Was Will's voice one of the shouts of agony I heard?

Or perhaps his dying groan was one of the ones that breached the quiet after the screams faded.

As the cheers from our enemy ship rose to the night sky.

I shudder, and for a moment I think it's over.

Stillness wraps me in her cloak and my head drops to the wood keeping me from the depths below.

Will is not here, but we succeeded.

In my memory I see his lip curled in his smirk of defiance.

"Let's go bring her home."

And we did. We brought Treasure home. He gave his life alongside me for the woman I loved.

And she doesn't know.

But wherever she is, she is safe.

I wish I could lay eyes on her one last time, but I don't wish she was here.

Keeping her safe during the battle would have been impossible. Not one man aboard my ship went into this battle with much of a chance.

Without naval experience she couldn't have known how poor our chances were.

She didn't know like Will and I did—that this was the likely end.

And I didn't tell her.

I kept her in the dark and sent her back to safety against her will.

The anger in her voice, the names she called me were all warranted for the lies I let her believe.

And I doubt she'll forgive me.

I draw a ragged breath as my side is pierced again.

If she could see me now, her eyes would not soften

with love the way they did days ago. Her full lips wouldn't tilt as she let out a breath, as the tightness of her shoulders relaxed.

She would not have given me her forgiveness.

She will never forgive me for abandoning her.

And yet, hers is the face I see as I draw what might be my last breath. As the pain throbs dully in my side, further away now. As if the pain is a dream, and *she* is real.

Her short, dark hair—more silken than the finest cloth under my fingers.

The lapping water is smooth and cold. The salt crusts on my lips.

But her skin is soft, warm in my hands, her lips pliable against mine.

The growing numbness fades, and I see the corners of her eyes crinkling with her smile—love shines in her eyes.

Love I threw away.

So she could live.

The bullet that grazed my ribs after the first cannonball hit the deck didn't leave a fatal wound. But submerged in the icy water, it's just a matter of time.

The sound of splintering wood ravages the air, and my eyes fall on the Lady Monroe just as her main deck breaks apart. Vibrations move through the water as the mast falls.

Water shoots up from where it slams into the surface.

The shriek abruptly cut off tells me I wasn't the sole survivor of my crew.

But now, I might be.

Lady Monroe has left me just like the woman I named her for.

Like I left the woman who taught my heart to beat again.

Like I left my Treasure.

And now…

It's too late.

CHAPTER 32

Tress

I reach my hand out for the leather-bound book. The wind against my face tastes like salt even before the tips of my fingers reach the surface of the cover.

The book we spent weeks looking for was the first thing I saw when I entered the basement. As if it can be found only when it chooses to.

The breeze in this empty room picks up, whipping my hair across my face.

I know Charles wouldn't want me to, and I know he might not want me anymore. Probably doesn't.

But I need to try.

For two excruciating weeks I've walked as a dead woman through my library responsibilities. My hands have catalogued, checked out, and ordered in books. But behind my pasted-on smile I have felt the shadow of loss streaking its discolored claws of empty into my skin, seeping its putrid stench into my veins.

And I can't bear it any longer.

The need to see him, to breathe in the scent of his skin, the mixture of aged leather and sea spray that will forever feel like home, burns through my soul.

I have left my post on the first floor where I should be. But instead I stand in the spot where I first saw him.

"Captain Charles William Seewell."

I feel the press of his lips against my knuckles.

And I need to see him again.

Need to know that Charles and his crew escaped the storm, that the impending battle never happened, that the Triangle of Spirits released the Lady Monroe.

I need to know he's safe.

Even if he never wants me.

My trembling fingers touch the leather cover and my fingertips burn.

I don't understand how the book works, and I doubt I ever will. I just need it to work for me one more time.

"Charles."

I whisper his name, as if the sound of it echoing off my lips can call him forth.

"I need to see you. I need to..."

I need to tell him.

That the words I threw at him in anger when he sat

272

me down on his desk aren't true. Never were and never could be true.

Regret burns in my chest as I recall them.

"I never loved you. I wish I'd never met you, I—"

The force of a gale plasters my hand to the book. I can't tear it away, even though my palm feels like it's on fire. My heart jolts with fear.

What if the book doesn't take me to Charles?

What if it doesn't take me to a ship at all? What if the battle he suspected is raging and I'm dropped into the middle of it?

The acrid smell of smoke hits my nostrils and the sound of crackling fire fills the air around me.

I pull my hand back, but it makes no difference, it's glued to the leather cover, and burning my skin.

Icy water soaks my Converse sneakers. My teeth chatter as I try to keep my mouth closed, waiting for the salt to burn my eyes as I'm pulled under the dark waters.

The book drops from my hand with a suddenness I don't expect, and I lose my footing.

My backside hits the carpeted concrete floor, and I yelp in pain.

My palm no longer burns. I hold it up in front of my face to see the skin pink and unharmed.

But I'm still in the library.

Despair pulls at me.

It didn't work.

I put my hands against the carpet soaked with sea water and push up to my feet.

The leather-bound book sits pathetically in a heap in the pool of receding seawater. I want to kick it.

I take another step towards the book ready to make good on my threat.

Slow, sluicing steps sound from behind me.

My heart stops.

I turn so fast the room spins for a minute, and then…

Piercing eyes meet mine, and I stop dead.

Anger radiates from the man stalking toward me. His gray eyes are near black with emotion, his face like a thundercloud.

My heart thunders in my chest as he closes the distance between us.

I've never seen a more terrifying sight than Charles Seewell stalking towards me, dripping wet and with murder in his eyes.

If I didn't believe him a bloodthirsty pirate before, I do now.

I believe him, because the rage I see in his eyes would make a smarter woman step back. Run away. Anything but what I do.

I step forward.

Charles.

I shape his name with my lips, but there's no breath to push the words into the air.

I've never seen a more beautiful sight than Charles Seewell, stalking towards me, dripping wet and with murder in his eyes.

He's here.

His wet clothes are stained with soot, and a large stain covers one side of his shirt.

His eyes narrow, and he grips my outstretched hand—his grasp on my fingers so hard it's painful. As if he's expecting my hand to fade before him. Expecting it to evaporate at his touch.

But I don't.

His eyes widen in shock.

His sharp intake of breath is the only sound in the room as he clasps my hand.

I can't take my eyes off of him.

His beautiful face is so pale, streaked with soot and sweat...and blood?

And I've never loved anything more.

His grip loosens around my hand. His cool thumb runs gently across my palm.

Shivers trail his touch, dancing their way up my nerve endings.

He stares from my hand to my face. As if he can't believe I'm here in the flesh.

But I am.

He is.

"Treasure."

His voice is raw, and goosebumps break out on my arms.

He repeats it like a prayer, like a plea. The reverence in his eyes makes my chest ache. My vision blurs.

"Treasure, are you here?"

I nod.

"I need to hear your voice."

"I'm here."

The voice that passes my lips sounds nothing like mine. It's too high pitched, too shaky. As if it no longer knows how to be.

Charles pulls on my arm until I'm off balance, and then he hauls me against his soaked chest.

He almost seems to wince at the impact, but then his arms are like steel bands around me. The force of his movements pushes the air from my chest until I gasp.

But his lips touch mine with the softness of butterfly wings.

CHAPTER 33

Tress

T"ress? Do you smell smoke? Is it coming from down here?"

The steady click-clack from Chris's heeled boots sound down the stairs as her voice comes closer, cutting through the haze of pleasure enveloping us.

Charles groans as he pulls away.

I turn to Chris whose eyes are trained on the arms still around my waist.

They flicker to the sopping wet carpet around us, and she closes her eyes briefly.

"Does time travel always cause water damage?"

But there's a smile lurking in her eyes belying the exasperation in her voice.

Charles's hands drop to my hips, then fall away completely.

He lets out another groan, but this time I don't mistake it for annoyance at being interrupted.

I turn back to face him, and alarm surges through me as he sways.

His skin is pale and graying, and his eyes are glassy and staring.

Chris lets out a startled cry.

"Tress, you're bleeding!"

But I'm not.

I look down to see the front and side of my sweatshirt soaked with a dark red stain.

"It's not my blood… Oh my God. Charles!"

He sways against me, and my feet move to disperse his weight, but he's too heavy.

He opens his mouth, but the words are slurred. I can't make out his garbled words, and he's crushing me with his weight.

"Chris, help me!"

She shoots forward, grabs his shoulder and helps me lower him to the floor.

"Where is he hurt?"

"I don't know!"

There's so much blood. His soaked shirt is suddenly blooming with red. The stain is everywhere. The metallic smell in the air turns my stomach. I watch helplessly as Charles's life seeps out of him.

Please, not now. I've just gotten him back!

"Don't you dare die on me!"

But Charles is slack-jawed and pale. And unconscious.

"Call 911!"

But Chris is already holding the phone to her ear.

I slide my finger along his jaw, and if I wasn't already kneeling, my knees would have buckled with relief.

"He has a pulse."

I move his lifeless arm to rest at an angle, push up his knee, and tilt him towards me.

"Male...in his thirties...major bleeding...no. I don't know. Tress, do you know of any medical conditions?"

I shake my head.

"He's from the 1700s, Chris, he's probably never even seen a doctor."

I let out a hysterical sound, halfway between a sob and a laugh.

Christ nods her head and relays the information to the dispatcher.

Minus the part about the 1700s.

"Clear airways, Tress. Tilt his chin up."

I follow her directions, cursing myself for not remembering.

Blood pounds in my ears and fear grips my stomach in a hold icier than death.

"I don't know. Tress, can you tell where the wound is? Chest or stomach?"

I pull at the soaked layers of fabric covering his body, but they are tucked too firmly into his pants. Curse the eighteenth century knee-length shirts!

My hands are stained red with blood and shaking, but I find the collar of his shirt and pull the ends apart. The fabric rips.

His skin is cool, and not a color that skin should have.

"Ribs! The wound is between his ribs."

"Pink blood?" Chris asks.

"No. No pink blood."

"Thank God."

I cover my hand with the sleeve of my sweatshirt and press the heel of my palm against the open wound.

"Can't they just send an ambulance?"

"They are on their way, sweetie. Is he still breathing?"

She leans close, but I'm already hovering the back of my hand over his mouth.

"He's breathing."

I let my fingers slide to his jaw.

"He's so cold."

Chris lets out a curse.

"He's probably got hypothermia... Yes, he's soaked in sea water...no... He might have been for a while, I don't know."

Sirens sound from outside, and it's the most beautiful sound I've ever heard.

"We're in the basement. Through the lobby, down the stairs."

Still pressing my hand against his ribs, I stroke his stubbled jaw with a hand sticky with his blood.

"You're going to make it, Charles. I love..."

But my voice breaks, and I taste the salt on my tongue.

"Don't leave me now. Please, don't leave me now."

Voices and commotion sounds on the stairs and in the next moment a flurry of activity descends upon the soaked basement.

A gentle hand lands on my shoulder. "Are you applying pressure to his wound?"

I nod, and the hand squeezes my shoulder. "That's good. You've done really good."

But I haven't done good. I should have realized that his movements were off, that his skin felt clammy.

A woman dressed in dark clothes kneels by Charles's head, and before I have enough time to wrap my head around what's happening, he's strapped to a stretcher being hauled up the stairs.

I follow as if in a daze until we're outside on the street.

He never moves.

The lights from the ambulance color his pale skin in hues of flashing red.

Please God, don't...

But I can't finish the prayer.

"Miss, are you a relation?"

"I'm his wife."

I feel Chris's eyes on me, but she doesn't rat me out. Instead she touches my shoulder, promising to meet me at the hospital. Her hand on my shoulder is warm, and safe, and steady.

And suddenly I'm so cold.

I shiver as I take a seat in the ambulance next to Charles. The EMTs clamp an oxygen mask over his face, and cover him with thin blankets.

He is so still.

I am so afraid.

"Please don't leave me."

I whimper the words, but he doesn't respond. His lips don't move, his eyelids don't flutter.

His response as he wrapped me in his arms minutes ago wasn't that of a man who'd willingly left me.

He didn't want me three weeks ago, I'm certain of that. Even as I tried to convince him in every way I could, he pushed me away, sent me back here, without as much as a *goodbye*.

And now he is back, and he wants me.

Or wanted me, until he collapsed.

The ambulance rolls to a stop. The doors open. More people crowd around us. Charles is wheeled out from the vehicle, and in through doors that lead to mint green and white corridors.

I follow behind him until gloved hands hold me back and the doors close behind his guernsey.

Separating us.

"He'll be in surgery, you'll be updated as soon as we know more."

A blue, nitrile gloved hand rests on my shoulder until I'm back in the waiting room.

I slide down onto a hard plastic seat.

I must be broken.

There's no way a heart can hurt this badly and still live, is there?

There can't be.

"Madam, can you fill this out to the best of your ability? Any information you have might be important."

A nurse holds out a clipboard to me.

With shaky fingers I write his name. But it's all I know. I don't even know his age.

I know his birth city, but not his medical history.

"I can't."

"Ma'am, your husband is in surgery, are you sure you don't have any more information? Does he have any underlying conditions? Do you have insurance?"

I shake my head, and I fall apart.

CHAPTER 34

Charles

Asort of squeaking fills my head as the dream world fades away from around me. The sound is loud and incessant. And more uniform than I've ever heard from a natural creature.

I don't like it.

There's a weird taste on my tongue, and I swallow trying to make it go away. My throat is parched.

As if I've gone days without water.

The pain hits me then—the side of my ribs burn as if they're being licked by flaming tongues of hell demons.

The bullet that tore through clothes and flesh during the battle. It hurt before, but nothing like this.

Did the wound in my side bring me to this place?

Is this purgatory?

The ache in my bones seems to point in that direction. As does the weakness in my limbs when I try to move. And the incessant noise.

My eyes are still closed, but the place I'm in must be bright. I sense the light against my closed eyelids, but I make no move to open them.

My chest burns as another, more crushing, pain fills it. I'm missing something—someone.

Treasure.

I'm missing Treasure.

After my injury I was with her again. She stood in front of me, hale and healthy. I reached out to touch her, and she didn't fade. I wrapped my fingers around hers, and still she was solid.

In my memory I take her in my arms. Press my lips to hers. Feel her respond. Hear her voice.

Was it a fever dream?

Or is this place eternity?

Was she an angel sent to lead me to purgatory?

But the way my body feels worn down to the bone, and the throbbing pain in my side, makes me think I am still in the natural world.

Perhaps not for long.

There is no strength in my limbs. As if I'm convalescing after a long sickness. Like the time I woke up in Merchant Monroe's house.

Is that where I am?

Did I somehow return to the past?

I can't be back in Sarah Monroe's house. She betrayed me, and she's not the woman I want. Not the woman I need.

The only woman I will ever need is the one I sent away when she professed her love for me.

The woman who is more treasure to me than gold and silver.

Desperate to know that the past is not where I am, I open my eyes.

I squint against the bright light from the lamps above me, and my head pounds with the small movement.

I close my eyes against the painful brightness.

A sudden scraping of metal rips through my head, and the pain is unbearable.

Then, the most beautiful voice says my name. Her voice is so full of relief it tugs at my heart.

"Charles!"

She's here.

What I glimpsed of the room, shades of white and stark light, looks nothing like her library, but my Treasure is here.

I open my eyes and my body sags with relief.

Her face is red, her eyes swollen, but her smile is brilliant—like glittering sunlight on a blue ocean. Her eyes sparkle, and then they well up with tears.

"I was so afraid for you."

Her voice is full of the tears that now overflow her eyes and run down her full cheeks.

She reaches out to touch me. Her soft hand slides along my cheek.

Her touch is heaven.

But her movements bring a new revelation. There are...cords?

Firm cords are attached to the inside of my nose. I lift my hand where another cord tugs the skin on top of my hand, as if it's threaded through me.

Panic rises in my chest.

What has happened to me?

Fear sparks in Treasure's eyes. Her hand ceases its path along my jaw.

"What is it?"

"The cords on my face?"

My voice is hoarse from disuse.

Her shoulders sag, and she closes her eyes for a moment.

"It's okay. You... You needed surgery and they needed to keep you safe. The cords were helping you breathe and keeping you asleep. They'll come take them off soon."

"Can you?"

There is no strength in my arms. I'm as weak as a cabin boy after his first storm. If I was a ship, the smallest squall would capsize me.

"I can't. I might hurt you if I tried."

I nod.

I don't want to cause her distress, but although she's no longer crying, she doesn't seem quite at ease.

I try to sit up, but weakness fills my bones.

Treasure rests a hand on my chest. "I don't think you should sit up yet. I'll call the nurse in here."

She presses a gray box sitting on the table next to me.

Her brown locks dance temptingly around her face as she moves.

I want to reach out and slide my fingers through them.

Curse the injury that has me confined to this bed!

Her eyes are glassy, and I think what I see in them is...longing?

For me?

"I was wrong, Treasure."

I push the words through my raw throat.

She sniffles, and when she speaks, there's a tremble in her voice.

"Were you though? You came back with a gunshot wound. What happened?"

"I wasn't…"

It takes effort to get the words out. The muscles in my abdomen ache as I push forth more words.

"…wrong to send you…"

I pull in another shaky breath.

"…away. But I didn't send you away because I didn't love you."

I'm shaking and my side burns worse than before.

But Treasure's sharp intake of breath, the hope suddenly filling her eyes, makes the pain worth it.

I look into eyes as blue as a windless sea, and I want to spend the rest of my life doing just that.

There's a flicker of emotion in the depths of her eyes.

I don't know exactly what it is, because suddenly the weight of the air around me seems to increase. Exhaustion flattens me like a heavy blanket.

I need to tell her why.

My eyelids flutter, and it takes effort to form the next words.

"I just did it to...keep you safe."

"I know."

Her warm fingers linger along my temple and the contact settles something deep in my chest. Something that's been a gaping hole since the moment I placed her on top of the book in my cabin and she vanished from between my arms.

Her touch is featherlight as she runs her fingertips over my ear and back down my jawline.

She's here and she's real, and it's all I need.

She's all I need.

"I'll be here when you wake up. Just rest."

Her voice seems to be coming from a distance, even though her fingers are still warm on my jaw.

I want her closer.

I want to stay with her, even as consciousness slips away from me, ragged bit by ragged bit.

My eyelids drop.

The light fades from around me, along with her soothing voice, and then her touch.

And I succumb to sleep.

CHAPTER 35

Tress

"You saved my life."

The raspy voice makes me look up from the pages of the book in my hands.

My limbs and neck ache as I slowly uncurl from the chair where I've been reading since Charles fell asleep hours ago.

The color of his skin is closer to his normal one, and his eyes are much more alert than they were then.

"I didn't know you were awake. Were you...watching me?"

The side of his mouth tugs upward in a smirk I've missed more than I've ever missed anything.

I drop the book onto the table next to me and take in the giant man in the hospital bed. The man I never thought I'd see again, and that I almost didn't.

My eyes burn and tears well up until it's like I'm looking at him through a veil of water.

A frown appears on his forehead.

"What's wrong?"

In the next moment, I'm by his side without knowing how I got there. I press my cheek to his neck, and my sobs are uncontrollable.

His large hands stroke my hair until I run out of tears.

I pull away far enough that I can see his face.

What I have to say to him, need to say to him, are words that must be said face to face.

"I didn't mean any of the things I said that day you sent me home. I just wanted to stay with you, and I thought you were making a mistake."

I was wrong about having run out of tears. Another trails down my cheek, dampening a spot of blanket on his chest.

"I was so angry at you. So angry that you refused to give us a chance."

His eyes are full of tenderness as he listens. He runs a finger down my cheek, trailing it along my jaw.

His touch calms me.

"I was so afraid you'd die and never know how I really felt about you."

A shadow crosses his face then.

"I almost did."

The chasm of loss opens up in my chest again, because he can't know yet how close he came. Even with today's medical knowledge, incurring hypothermia after an injury is often fatal.

I clasp my hand over his, needing to know it's here, clasping me back.

I remember again as he stalked toward me after the book called him forth yesterday. He didn't appear hurt then. But he must have already been.

"What happened before the book brought you back to me?"

The shade that settles in his eyes reminds me of grief.

"We lost the Lady Monroe."

The flatness of his words holds a world of pain. One I wish I could ease. But grief cannot be corralled into comfort.

"What about Will?"

Visions of the Lady Monroe's First Mate with the boyish grin plays in my head. Will is the man Charles trusted to take care of me when we went ashore in Newport. The one who walked with him onto their first ship to beg for work.

But Charles shakes his head.

"The whole crew was lost. I think I was the only one left."

My heart smarts. The men he worked with must have been a great loss. But the man I know he considered a brother?

"I'm so sorry."

I don't know how to ease his pain, but I want to so desperately.

I lean forward and brush a kiss to his dry lips.

"I love you. I'm so sorry for your pain."

He closes his eyes, as if it hurts too much to keep them open. Or maybe he is still exhausted from the surgery.

"I was in the water. I watched the Lady Monroe burn next to one of the other ships."

He pulls in a ragged breath.

"I was shot near the beginning of the battle, and must have been losing blood for a while."

"So if I hadn't called you back...?"

I know what he's saying, but I can't say the words out loud. Can't even think them.

How could I have been gone from him for three weeks and have him appear straight from the battle that must have happened no later than sunset the same day I left?

If our time lines had matched, he would have been...

No. I can't.

Not now that I can see him with my eyes, run my hands over his face and neck. Clasp his hand and feel the returning squeeze of his fingers.

"I waited almost a month."

He groans without opening his eyes. "You weren't gone a month, Treasure."

"Maybe not. But it's been three weeks for me in my world."

His eyes open, they're not as clear as before. As if he's stayed awake too long already.

"Why did you call me back?"

"Because I couldn't bear the thought of you not knowing how I really felt. Meeting you when you came through the book the first time was the best thing that's ever happened to me. Even those three weeks. I couldn't eat or sleep. I cried until I had no more tears. I thought you hated me."

A faint smile plays on his lips.

"I never hated you."

"I thought that I was the only one that fell in love."

"I love you Treasure."

The words are staccato and weak, but they are the most beautiful words I've ever heard.

I lean over him and press my lips to his forehead. His cheekbones. His lips.

"You saved my life...when you called me back."

His eyes flutter shut, and he's asleep.

I may have saved his life by using the book to call him back yesterday. But I think we both know that he saved mine first.

I pull his hand to my lips and kiss his knuckles.

"You saved mine."

Captain Charles William Seewell saved me in every way I needed to be saved. He saved me from my predictable existence ensconced behind my books. From the ivory tower of fiction where I lived safely separate from love.

I tried to shut the doors on heartbreak and abandonment, but instead I shut out the life I really wanted.

My old rule of life resounds in my head.

Life is unpredictable, but fiction?

Fiction is not.

And yet, I'd choose this unpredictable man over each and every one of my fictional heroes.

Not because he is perfect.

Far from it.

But the love in his eyes as he looks at me? The sacrifice he made to protect me? None of my books have ever done that for me.

Jonah was wrong.

So was Eon, my parents, and Lucas.

I am worth staying for.

Worth sacrificing, and waiting for.

Love is for me.

And none of these are fairy tales.

EPILOGUE

Tress

The Atlantic Ocean, seven months later

Placid waves thump against the hull of the ship far beneath us. The rhythmic sound like an echo of my heart.

Mine, and the one beating in time with it against my back.

Charles's arm tightens around me, anchoring me firmly to his chest. And there's nowhere else I'd rather be.

Not anywhere but where I can feel his heart beat, strong and alive against my back.

Nowhere else but where I can watch the ocean spread out in front of us, as far as the eye can see. Bright blue, and with May sunlight turning the frothy white foam gathering atop each wave into sparkling diamonds.

It's beautiful and ethereal, and entirely deceiving of the destructive powers we both know the ocean hides beneath its billowing surface.

Behind me, Charles's chest rises and falls with a sigh of contentment. It's a sound I'll never grow tired of. And one that never fails to appear when his feet are on the deck of a ship, where his constant wide stance belongs.

Thankfully, this little New England town we both call home has an abundance of ships similar to the ones he used to sail.

Like the one we're on right now.

There are perks to living next door to a bustling eighteenth century seaport museum, and one of them is a paid job for a man whose knowledge of these ships more than rivals that of modern-day historians.

"One day we'll have a ship again."

His laugh rumbles against my back, and my toes curl in my boots.

"Have you ever bought a ship before, Mrs. Seewell? They're quite costly."

The sound of the name that is finally mine makes my heart speed up and sends thrills through my stomach.

"I haven't. But my husband once lost one because of me, and I want to make it up to him."

Sorrow casts a shadow over the moment as I remember all he lost to keep me safe.

His lifelong friend. His crew. In some ways, his whole world.

"I'd make the trade all over again."

His voice is husky and low, and goosebumps break out across my skin as his breath warms my neck.

"I still want you to have a ship. To teach your sons."

Both his arms wrap around me before his hands trail over the substantial bump straining the fabric of my dress—where more hearts beat.

Hearts that are part of both of us.

For two people who waited what seemed like a lifetime to meet, we haven't waited long for anything else.

The Doppler ultrasound that picked up two little heartbeats back in March threw us for a loop, but the ultrasound a month later that showed two little boys growing inside me, didn't.

We've already named them.

Eon Hayden Seewell and William Hayes Seewell.

After the brothers we both lost.

Eon still lives, as far as I know, somewhere, but buried under the weight of his addiction, it's been more than a year and a half now since I've heard his voice.

Maybe one day he'll come home and be an uncle to my children. Or perhaps he won't.

Will never will.

Sorrow edges in at the corners of my chest, and I close my eyes tightly against the memories.

It's been a long year, brimming with grief. But I wouldn't trade this moment. Wouldn't trade this new chance at life, for both of us.

I used to think love and loss could be avoided. That if I pushed love away, loss would never have the power to hurt me.

But instead I kept the loss alone, every aching, blood-stained ounce of it, and pushed away the one thing that made it bearable.

I lean back against Charles's solid chest. The sun's heat warms my skin, it's light drawing my eyes to the dancing sparkles it creates in the thick, intricate pattern of the gold band on my finger.

"Two bodies, one heart."

The inscription is old, maybe even older than the band itself. Sewn into Charles's shirt, this ring is the only personal artifact he saved when the Lady Monroe went down.

A few short weeks after he was released from the hospital, he gave it to me and asked me to keep it.

"On the condition that you stay with me forever."

He didn't need to ask twice, and I dressed in a white gown for him two weeks later.

And promised him all the days of my life.

I spent too many years, too many precious days of mine pushed aside by the people I loved. People who scarred my heart so badly it bled at the lightest prod. Enough to make me cling only to the stories that made me feel safe.

I pulled away from a life that battered me when I tried to love it, and made a home for myself within the pages of stories meant for entertainment.

Until Captain Charles William Seewell stepped out of one of the books in the old sandstone library where I worked, and made me reconsider.

I turn in that same man's embrace, the movement a bit more complicated now than twenty weeks ago, and catch his gray eyes as they move from the ocean before us to connect with mine.

Butterflies take off in my stomach, and I'm not sure if it's the way he looks at me or the sudden bubble-burst movement of one of his sons in my abdomen.

I bite my lip, and his eyes drop to where my teeth pull on it.

"Your boys are moving."

They always move when I'm aboard a ship.

His eyes flip to mine again, and a grin spreads on his bronzed face.

"They know they belong at sea."

Like their father.

Their father whose forehead is touching mine. Whose mouth presses to mine in the softest, most perfect of kisses.

And I know that this moment was worth the heart-ache.

Our story, and even our day-to-day lives, may not be predictable.

It's not fiction.

But it's real and it's life.

And, best of all?

It's mine.

THE END

AUSTIN RYAN

A Note from the Author

Thank you for reading this story, I hope you enjoyed reading it as much as I enjoyed writing it. If you loved it, or just liked it, I hope you'll consider leaving a review on Amazon or Goodreads. Thank you!

Also available from Austin Ryan

The Triangle of Spirits Series:
Pirate's Treasure (Book 1)
Mermaid's Tale (Book 2) Coming 2022

Norwegian Heritage Series:
The Christmas Marriage Plot

Acknowledgements

I wrote the bulk of this book back in 2019, and when I stumbled over the half-finished manuscript at the end of this summer, I just couldn't put it down.

This story, with all it's whimsy and poetry and heartache, called to me, and oh, how I've loved answering.

While this is a pirate story, and a love story, it's also a love letter to the Atlantic Ocean—I grew up on one coast and have lived most of my adult life on the other.

The ocean has been awe and wonder and steadfastness to me, in a season when I struggled to see it elsewhere.

But, while I might have written most of this book in actual solitude, I didn't write it alone. If you're one of the people who helped this book become what it is, I'm beyond thankful to you.

Most of all, I'm thankful to God—for the people, places, and skills that made me able to write this book.

Many thanks also to:

My grandmother, Farmor—for the time you told me about your first attempt at sewing a velvet dress without knowing that velvet was a terrible fabric to work with, but you attempted it anyway. I think about you, and that story, every time I need the courage to try. And I've needed it a lot this year. I miss you always.

My son, Kieran—for your marketing advice and encouragement, and all your help brainstorming. For sitting across the table from me, smirking. I am so incredibly lucky to be your Mama, and to get to call you mine. I love you always.

Jenni Sauer—for everything. You are my serotonin and my rock, and the constant bringer of sense to my world.

Tara Knott—for always making sure I lock the doors, blow out my candles, and eat. For being a Queen of Blankets and a World Treasure, and for the gift of your amazing friendship. You are my sanity.

Lauren Wyant—for being my Emotional Support Person through crises big (hurricanes) and small (too numerous to mention). You are incredible, I could never have made it through this year without you.

Leeah Fisher—May your fangs be strong and never bend, and if they do, may you always have friends by your side willing to hunt for you. I love you always.

My Virtual Roommate, Ingjerd Løvgren Auestad—for inspiring this book with your librarian woes, I'm sure you remember me asking what you'd do if you found a soaked person in the basement at the library. Also, we're out of pasta sauce.

My UnWriters (Cat Wiant, Amanda Johnson, Jenny Baldwin, Leeah Fisher, Vicky Esquivel, Amanda Thornell, Kayleigh Wilkes, Desarae Wisnoski, and Tara Knott)— Writing and publishing alongside all of you has been more rewarding than I ever could have imagined.

Selina R. Gonzalez—for using your magical formatting skills to make this book look so beautiful on the inside.

Cat Wiant— for your unwavering support of me and this book. You have no idea how much it means to me (but the continued lack of flowers and cowboys should give you an idea).

Karen Maston—for your prayers and wisdom, and for always encouraging my writing.

Kaylie Plumb—for your amazing, professional Marine Linguist insight into the habits of ocean dwellers, and for your friendship. I do believe in science, I do, I do.

Author Colleen Hoover—for letting me use my favorite *Heart Bones* quote in this book, and for writing so many of my favorite books.

My editor, Savanna Roberts—You have been an absolute delight to work with. You cracked down on every weakness in this story (and the numerous strange autocorrect typos) and brought out every strength, all while not reducing me to a pile of soggy tears. I can't thank you enough.

Marie, our imaginary kitchen maid—for always leaving me to clean up the kitchen. Actually, thanks for nothing, Marie.

About the Author

AUSTIN RYAN was born and raised in Norway, after years of finding her happiness in books, spending every spare hour in an old library, and staring wistfully out at the ocean, she accidentally wrote a novel about a modern day librarian falling in love with a 18th century pirate. Pirate's Treasure is her first full-length novel.

Austin lives in Connecticut, surrounded by overflowing bookshelves, Christmas lights, and sparkly things.

When she is not editing words for other authors, getting lost in their stories, or writing her own, you can find her on adventures with the best son in the world, warming the bleachers at his football games, and spending hours down by the ocean.

Connect with Austin at AustinRyanWrites.wordpress.com or on Facebook, Instagram, Amazon, or Goodreads.